1 | Page

Merci of the Gods

Copyright.

All rights reserved. No part of this book may be reproduced, distributed, or transmitted in any form or by any means, including photocopying, recording, or other electronic or mechanical methods, without the prior written permission of the author, except in the case of brief quotations embodied in critical reviews and specific other noncommercial uses permitted by copyright law.

TXu2-404-603 December 27, 2023.

Dedication

This book is dedicated to Gloria Dubignon Shine, my loving mother, who I miss daily. I did it, Mom! To my son, Guy, to my daughters, Serria and Saadika, for their support. And my God brother, Stoney Mallory, for making me angry enough to finish.

Table of Contents

Introduction

As Ninhursag finished her last experiment of the day, she noticed that the Royal DNA column was glowing brightly, *but why?* She thought to herself, *I must tell the king.* Ninhursag rushed into the king's chambers so out of breath and hardly able to speak. "Great One," she said, "an extra strand has suddenly appeared in the Royal DNA column."

The king gave her a look that sent chills down her spine, but still, she continued, "A female royal heir is about to come of age, but none have been born into the royal line for thousands of years. The strand can only change when a female royal gives birth to another female who is coming of age, creating a continuum in the royal column."

The king replied sharply, "You say this as if I need a lesson on the royal DNA column." Ninhursag, who was Anu's Chief Medical officer, looked confused, so the king sent for Enlil, his Chief Scientist, and together, they assured Anu that their experiments had created nothing that would affect the royal DNA column in this way. Enraged, the king dismissed them, then he called for the Hallaku of the seventh house and sent a messenger to the leader of the

Sebittu. "I will find and destroy you," he roared, and the heavens trembled.

Chapter 1: Estelle

Estelle A Lowe was widely regarded as the top linguist and most sought-after archaeologist in the world. Her exceptional talent lay in translating any and all ancient languages as if she had spoken them in another life. Her profound understanding of the ancients, their culture, religion, and way of life, along with her respect for the people, made her the best.

Estelle always took special care of the artifacts, as if she were caring for her own personal belongings. Currently, Estelle is on the excavation site of the ancient city of Ur, one of the known cities of the Ancient Sumerian civilization. She had been searching for this for an eternity, as it was the key to her lifelong work.

One night, while working late, Estelle heard what sounded like a baby crying in the distance. Laughing to herself, she said, "Too long in the desert," returning to her work. Again, she heard it and decided to follow the sound. It was pitch black, and the only light was the reflection of the moon in the darkness. But she continued to follow the sound as if in a trance. As she reached the excavation site, she stopped, listening for the sound again. Entering, she realized the cries were coming from within the tunnel. She wondered why a baby would be there. The cries grew louder and louder as she approached until she saw a young woman crouched in the corner. Raising her hands, she handed Estelle the baby as if it were an offering to the gods.

Estelle held the baby close, panicking, looking around to find something to wrap the naked baby in. It was very cold and damp in the tunnel, but when she turned back around, the woman was gone. All Estelle could remember was her eyes. Those familiar eyes. In the weeks that followed, an investigation was conducted, but neither the young woman nor anyone who knew her could be found.

Consequently, the child was taken to an orphanage in Iraq. All Estelle could think of was that beautiful baby in an orphanage; she was not going to let that happen. Estelle began to reason with herself as to how to prevent it. The sensible thing would be to let someone else handle it, but all she remembered was those cat eyes that touched her soul.

Feeling responsible for this baby, she knew she had to do something, but what? The question: what would she do with a baby? Estelle decided to take matters into her own hands, so she adopted the child. She knew it would not be easy because she was always traveling the world, and her schedule was hectic, but she was determined to make it work. She wanted to give this child a good life and ensure her work did not interfere with her duties as a mother.

As she adjusted to motherhood, Estelle found herself facing a new challenge of balancing work and parenting responsibilities. However, she was determined to give this little girl, whom she named Merci, the best life possible. She would take Merci along with her on adventures, exposing her to new cultures and languages with the help of her colleagues and her neighbor, Miss Fisher. They survived.

Estelle's love for her daughter, Merci, was unyielding; she wanted her daughter to experience a life filled with excitement and thrill. Together, they traveled the globe, exploring exotic and breathtaking places. Merci developed a passion for archeology, which Estelle fostered by providing her with a small dig kit to play with while she worked. By the time Merci turned seven, Estelle was highly sought after by archaeologists from all corners of the world; the discovery of new sections of the city of Ur had been made, and the professor in charge specifically requested Estelle's presence. Without hesitation, Estelle and Merci embark on yet another adventure. After spending several weeks at the excavation site, it was almost time for Estelle and Merci to return to the United States and for Merci to return to school.

One evening, as Estelle was returning to their tent, she overheard voices, including one that she could not quite place. Upon entering the tent, her world came crashing down as she recognized those eyes as Merci's birth mother. Estelle and the woman stepped outside to talk, and when Estelle returned to the tent, she was alone. Merci asked her about the woman. Estelle tried to downplay the situation, but she knew that her life and Merci's life were about to change drastically.

One day in the future, she would tell Merci the story of a special little girl, but for now, she just wanted to shield her from the harsh realities of the world. Once they had arrived home and unpacked their bags, Estelle surprised Merci by giving her a state-of-the-art telescope, and from then on, Merci would spend nights gazing at the sky. "Bedtime, young lady; you have a trip tomorrow," Estelle reminded her as she walked into her room, which was cluttered with books and papers. Merci loved school, especially science, and she was excited about the class trip to the Hayden Planetarium the next day. She couldn't sleep because of her excitement. Merci loved the sky and often drew different constellations in her notepads; her favorite constellations were Orion's Belt and the Little Dipper. The Stars seemed to call out to her, and she always responded in awe. When Estelle looked up, Merci was heading towards her, over her mess of books and papers, answering, "Yes, Mom, what is it?"

"Is everything okay?"

"Yes," Merci said as she reached over and gave her mom a good night kiss.

"Wow, that was the first," said Estelle.

That night, Merci had dreams of angels and stars. In Her Dream, she met an angel named N2. This celestial being was breathtakingly beautiful, resembling the goddesses from the movies Merci loved to watch. N2 was adorned in a resplendent gold and white gown, her hair crowned with gold. Her smile illuminated the sky. Strangely, she kept addressing Merci as the light of the world despite Merci's attempts to correct her by stating her name. The dream left Merci in a state of perplexity.

"Time to get up and get ready for your trip," Estelle called out, breaking the reverence of Merci's dream. Without missing a beat, Merci leaped out of bed and dressed in record time. Her mother looked astonished by how quickly she was ready.

"Wow, that's quick," she remarked.

As they headed towards the school, Merci couldn't stop talking about the angel she had encountered in her dream. She was so absorbed in her story that her mom struggled to get a word in edgewise. Merci's excitement and curiosity were palatable.

Upon arriving at the school, they saw lines of buses being loaded with what seemed like dozens of children. Merci eagerly rushed towards the bus where her teacher, Miss Hunter, awaited. "Hello, Miss Hunter," she acclaimed, skipping the first step onto the bus. Estelle greeted Mrs. Hunter and settled into the seat next to Merci. The anticipation in the air was tangible as the buses lined up, ready to transport the students to the planetarium. Once the buses had parked and the children began to disembark, the atmosphere was buzzing with excited chatter. No one seems to be paying much attention to the teachers. Miss Hunter, one of the fifth-grade teachers, tried to restore order. "Line up, everyone," she called out, counting each child as they left the bus.

However, amidst the excitement, the kids were more focused on their conversations and surroundings. Mrs. McIntosh, the principal, raised her voice to get their attention, "For those of you who are not listening, get back on the bus. If you're not going to behave now while we're outside, I refuse to allow any of you to go inside!" The threat worked like magic because suddenly, all the children stood in a straight line, paying close attention. Principal McIntosh organized the children into groups.

Estelle, being one of the parent chaperones, took charge of a group of kids that included Merci, Sky, Sariah, Fatima, Jason, Tariq, and Guy. These youngsters were amongst the brightest in the fifth grade. Estelle had a fantastic time with them. What set this group apart was their inquisitiveness. They didn't ask the typical questions kids their age might ask; instead, they were fascinated by how much Estelle knew.

As they eagerly moved between the exhibits, Estelle could see they were thoroughly enjoying the experience. "Mama, can we go to the IMAX theater?" Merci asked, running in that direction with the other children following suit. They all clamored into the chairs just in time for the sky show. Their young minds absorb the knowledge like sponges, learning a lot about the sky and the stars. With the best chaperone, Dr. Lowe, having the opportunity to acquire valuable insight into how the cosmos work. As they explore the planetarium and learn more about the planets, their atmospheres, and the vastness of the universe, the children are captivated by the wonders of space.

Estelle, being the thoughtful chaperone, decided to treat them to a visit to the souvenir shop before they returned to the buses, allowing each child to pick out something of their choice. Merci, true to her nature, opted for a book titled Planet X, while the other children chose toys, stickers, and various trinkets. Merci's hunger for knowledge led her to this book.

At the end of the trip, the girls gathered around Fatima, Merci's next-door neighbor, who was her closest friend. She was raised by her grandmother because, tragically, her mother had been murdered just 6 months after Fatima's birth. Rumors circulated around the neighborhood that her boyfriend was responsible for her murder, and there were speculations about whether he or one of her numerous friends could be Fatima's father. It was a grim story that

Fatima had grown up with, a reminder of the harsh realities of their neighborhood. Fatima often pretended not to care about her family's complications, complicated history, and the circumstances of her birth. Beneath that tough exterior, she was just a little girl dealing with a lot.

With that tough exterior, she sometimes acted a bit older than her age, trying to navigate the complexities of life in their neighborhood. Despite the hardships, Merci and Fatima's friendship was unwavering, offering them both a sense of support and understanding in a challenging environment.

Sariah, often known as Yaya, was the only daughter in her family of three children. She resided at 8 Morningside Avenue. 115th Street in Harlem, New York. In the order of birth, Sariah fell right in the middle, having one older brother and one younger. Unfortunately, her older brother frequently found himself in trouble in the neighborhood, leading to repeat encounters with law enforcement. This constant cycle of misbehavior often landed him in jail, causing distress for their family. Sariah's mother worked hard to manage the local supermarket, just around the corner from their home. While her father struggled with alcoholism, often resorting to violence within their household.

Sky, on the other hand, was introduced to Merci when she was 10 years old, and they were both in the fifth grade. Although she lived uptown, she attended the same school as Merci, Eastside Prep.

Sky's father held the position of pastor at the Open Arms chapel and sanctuary; their family was deeply committed to community service. Specializing in assisting the homeless and those in need. Sky's mother was equally dedicated and operated an organization called Women Against Crack from the church's basement. Their mission was to make a positive impact on the inner city by offering free food and housing assistance to anyone requiring help. Despite her devotion to the cause, Sky found it irksome when people labeled her as PK, short for preacher's kid, as it felt restrictive and didn't reflect her true identity. Since that day at the planetarium, these four girls had become inseparable.

They spent all their time together, studying and playing as a tight-knit group. Their friendship provided solace and a sense of belonging, offering something to look forward to amidst the challenges of their lives. They especially love visiting Merci's house because they adore Mama Lowe, as they affectionately call her. She made them feel loved, welcome, and at ease, not to mention that her kitchen was always stalking delicious food and treats.

When Merci and Mama Lowe would embark on the expeditions and archaeological digs, the girls genuinely missed them. Merci had spent a significant part of her youth traveling to distant places with her mother; they had been to Bimini, and the Bahamas, Mexico City, Egypt, Costa Rica, Turkey and had explored the ruins of Troy. They also ventured as far as Easter Island in the South Pacific. Sometimes, they were away for a year or even longer.

Estelle Aristarr Lowe, or Dr. Lowe as she was known professionally, held a remarkable educational background; she possessed a PhD from Harvard University in linguistics, another PhD in astrophysics, a master's degree in anthropology, and a doctrine from Yale University in archeology. She was the go-to expert for anything related to ancient civilizations, astronomy, and the mysteries of the ancient world.

Estelle's primary scholarly fascination revolved around ancient Sumerians, and she had conducted her graduate thesis on the subject, which delved into the intricate topic of the ancient Sumerians and the gods believed to have ascended from the heavens. One of her specialties was cuneiform, the written language of the ancient Sumerians. She began teaching Merci about cuneiform form from a young age, employing an inventive game to facilitate learning. Letters and words were on index cards, and then she would challenge Merci to select a card based on its meaning. This playful approach allowed Merci to connect meanings with cuneiform symbols, effectively teaching her how to translate the ancient script without her even realizing it.

Estelle was meticulously preparing Merci for something significant, something that would one day become very clear to her—hoping that Merci would eventually comprehend her intentions and willingly carry on her research. She believed that she had instilled in Merci a profound love for archeology. While most little girls her age were preoccupied with different interests, Merci's head was always in the clouds. She's curiously consumed books about Planet X, also known as Nibiru, including the works of authors like Zachariah Stitchins. One of her favorites was Chariot of the Gods by Eric von Daniken. Merci loved science fiction and archeology.

Estelle was determined to provide Merci with a well-rounded education, particularly as she was about to turn 16. At this age, Merci began to inquire about her mother and father; she was aware only of her adoption by Estelle. These questions about her true identity and why her biological parents had left her were increasingly pressing, and she yearned for answers.

Estelle dreaded the inevitable day when she would have to address Merci's persistent questions about her biological parents. She wasn't sure how much longer she could dodge the truth, and she hoped her evasions would suffice. The one thing she was certain of was her deep love for Merci, and she didn't want to ever lie to her. Yet she had made a solemn promise to keep Merci safe at all costs. Her conversation with Merci's mother had shed light on the significance of a wooden box Merci would someday be entrusted with. Inside it was the key—a key that was meant for Merci. Estelle guarded it with her life until the day and time it was to be presented to Merci, never realizing its ultimate importance.

Chapter 2: Merci

The beginning of December 2006 approached, and Merci's birthday was only a few weeks away. Her mother had received an invitation to travel to Cambridge, England, to teach class at the prestigious Cambridge University. This was an exciting time for England. The country had recently celebrated its victory over Ecuador in the World Cup, and they were in the midst of a fervent breastfeeding debate. Cricket in England was also experiencing a revival. The anticipation in the midst of all of this was palpable; it was an exciting moment to visit this vibrant nation.

Given that school would soon be out on break for Christmas, Estelle decided to temporarily withdraw Merci from her classes. Her advanced academic progress meant she wouldn't fall behind, and besides, she had a knack for returning with captivating stories from her adventures.

So, off to England, they went, ready for new experiences in their lives. The Christmas holiday was in full swing. All the shops along Carnaby Street in London were festively decorated. Even though Estelle didn't celebrate Christmas, she appreciated it. In Estelle's view, Christmas was akin to many of the holidays rooted in pagan traditions.

Given her extensive historical knowledge, she believed that it had become a way for the rich to grow richer and the poor to spend money they could not afford. It puzzled her why people went into debt during this season, to struggle for the rest of the year to pay off that debt. This was confounding, considering that historical records didn't support the idea that Jesus was born on December 25th, and Estelle knew better.

Cambridge was stunning this time of year. The city's architecture was a magnificent presence in itself, and the snow-covered landscape added to the serene atmosphere. Merci observed the people bustling about, engaged in the everyday affairs of life as if her soul had found peace, a place of welcoming and serenity.

"Honey," Estelle said, "we're going to check into the Travelodge at Leisure Park until our temporary home is ready."

"Okay, that sounds great," replied Merci.

She was truly excited not just for their stay at Cambridge, but the prospect of visiting London, a mere 50 minutes away from Cambridge, filled Merci with bubbling excitement. London, the capital of both Europe and the United Kingdom, was a sprawling metropolis brimming with history and modernity. As they ventured to London, the Tower of London stood tall on the North Bank of the River Thames, casting its awe-inspiring shadow over Central London. Merci couldn't help but be mesmerized by its grandeur, thinking about the countless stories and secrets it held within its historic walls.

Their day in London was a whirlwind of discovery. Merci and Estelle explored iconic landmarks like Madame Tussauds, where wax figures of celebrities and historical figures came to life before their very eyes. They stood in front of the regal Buckingham Palace, imagining the grandeur of the royal ceremonies that happened there. The site of Big Ben towering above brought about a sense of reverence for the passage of time and the city's rich history.

As the day grew to a close, they embarked on the journey back to Cambridge. The evening painted the sky with vibrant colors as the sun dipped below the horizon. Merci's heart swelled with a profound appreciation for the beauty of life. She felt incredibly fortunate to have Estelle as her mother—a person she loved more than words could ever express. Estelle, an accomplished scholar who had taught at esteemed institutions such as Berkeley University in New

York City and NYU, was no stranger to the world of academia.

She had a remarkable gift for teaching, specializing in languages like Sanskrit, cuneiform, and hieroglyphics. Her passion for ancient civilizations and languages was contagious, and Merci had inherited her mother's love for exploration, as well as her constant quest for knowledge. Back in Cambridge, Merci was eager to explore the famed university. She spent an entire day traversing the historic campus, taking in its impressive architecture.

The Fitzwilliams museum left her in awe with its colossal white columns, reminiscent of ancient Rome. She couldn't help but wonder about the influence of Roman architecture in Cambridge. As she strolled through the campus, Merci marveled at buildings like The Corpus Christi building and the more modern Churchill College. Among these architectural wonders, Trinity Hall stood out as the most captivating, especially when the morning sunbathed it in a warm, golden light. Merci found herself pondering how many remarkable individuals had passed through these hallowed halls. Merci's mind went to the crazy, sometimes dangerous neighborhood that she and her friends lived in, realizing that few of them had ever or would ever witness the breathtaking beauty she was experiencing now.

Wanting to share this Wonder with her friends and neighbors, resolving to bring back pictures, stories, and perhaps even a piece of magic itself, her enthusiasm was boundless. That night, beneath a blanket of stars, Merci delved into a recurring dream that felt like an equal adventure. She soared high above an ancient city, feeling the wind rush past her as she looked down upon people living their lives below. The setting was so vivid, depicting both simple huts and grand structures, some still under construction.

Intriguingly, Merci observed what appeared to be an intricate irrigation system. She wanted to reach out to these distant souls, to communicate with them, but her voice couldn't bridge the gap between her world and theirs. The people below moved about, oblivious to her presence in their ancient landscape. Awakened by the sound of her mother's voice, "Merci," she was jolted from this dreamlike Revere, questioning the urgency of a bus that she had forgotten about.

Her mom gently reminded her that they were embarking on an extraordinary journey. Estelle's archeology class was venturing to the Iranian desert to contribute to the excavation of the ancient city of Nippur. The existence of this has been traced back to around 5,000 BC. The air buzzing with anticipation, Merci and her mother joined a group of 20 students from various divisions within the university's archeology department as they departed.

Cambridge's excitement radiated from the other students, but Merci's demeanor seemed somewhat subdued. Sitting down beside her daughter on the plane, Estelle quickly addresses the unease, "Honey, what's wrong? I thought you'd be thrilled about this expedition. Merci!"

Estelle called out. Merci's expression, a mix of excitement and fatigue, she answered, "I am excited; it's just that I haven't been sleeping well recently." "Merci," Estelle said, concerned, inquiring more, "why haven't you mentioned this before?" Merci explained in a loving tone, "I didn't want to worry you." Determined to ensure her daughter's well-being, Estelle said firmly, "All right, the first chance we get, you're going to the doctor, okay?" Merci agreed with a respectful "yes, ma'am" and then attempted to catch some much-needed rest during the flight.

Estelle observed her daughter as she slept, noting the telltale signs of adolescents. Merci was on the brink of her

16th birthday, and the changes were already underway. Her beauty had evolved. Her once-long hair now cascaded way down her back. Her captivating almond cat eyes seem to grow more enchanting by the day. Estelle's baby girl was growing up as well, nearly matching her mother's height. Her birth mother's prophecy had claimed that at 16, her questions would outnumber answers, but it was at 21 that Merci would fully come into her own.

Estelle's duty was to protect her until then—a responsibility that she took seriously and accepted willingly. Upon arriving at the excavation site, Merci had the opportunity to meet a diverse group of people in the crowd. She also forged new friendships, now expanding her circle. This was not the first class that Estelle had taught; she had tenure at Berkeley University in New York City as well as NYU. Whenever she was in New York for any length of time, she had a permanent class at NYU teaching Sanskrit, cuneiform, and hieroglyphics.

For Merci, her days at the excavation site were a mix of schoolwork and practical learning. Graduation from high school was fast approaching, and she was diligently preparing for her regions and her SAT exams. Excelling in these tests was crucial to her, as they would open the door to prestigious colleges. With ambitions set high, Merci aimed for top scores that would grant her access to the best colleges and universities in the world. The determination to succeed drove her to study rigorously, ensuring she had her pick of higher education institutions.

Once the Sun dipped below the horizon, Merci transitioned from the classroom to the field. In the evening, she would assist Estelle and her students in sorting through the excavated soil and the day's findings. They uncovered a trove of artifacts, including pottery shards, although nothing of great significance yet. This hands-on experience and Estelle's classes allowed her to learn alongside the students, a privilege that placed her ahead of the curve when she started college.

Nippur had been excavated repeatedly over the years. Merci began wondering what they expected to find, given the extensive prior explorations. Her musings were abruptly interrupted by a sudden downpour. The rain halted all excavation work for the day. It was an unusual occurrence since it rarely rained in this region. The following day brought a bright sunrise, revealing the ruins of this powerful, advanced civilization. Merci stepped out into the sunlight and, to her astonishment, there before her was the great City of Nippur and all its grandeur.

She blinked, half expecting the city to disappear like a mirage, and then she glanced around to see if others were witnessing the same miracle. Merci could hardly contain her emotions as she muttered out loud, "It's, it's the city I've seen in my dreams."

As she continued towards the magnificent site, half believing she was in another dream. What baffled her was the stark contrast inside the ruins; Nippur was pulsing with life, its grander evident. Yet when she turned back towards the camp, all that remained was a pile of ruins.

Later that night, after everyone had retired to their tents, Merci felt an irresistible urge to return to the ruins. What unfolded next was beyond extraordinary. She walked through the streets of this ancient city, a place that existed over 5,000 years ago, and yet, here she was, experiencing it vividly. The city was bustling with activity. EnLil's Temple was under construction, and Merci ventured inside it as if she had stepped into a different world. It was beautiful, filled with golden statues and fragrant incense. It was as if she had stepped back in time, immersed in an alternate reality.

"Wow," she thought. Then, just as she became immersed in this surreal experience, she felt a touch on her shoulder. Turning around, her mother stood there, "Baby, are you okay?"

"Yes, mama," Merci replied, "Do you see that?" pointing towards the temple she had just left. But when Estelle looked, it had vanished.

"Oh, see what?" her mother inquired.

Puzzled, Merci waved it off, dismissing the peculiar incident. Throughout the day, Merci couldn't stop thinking about how incredible the experience had been. It felt as if she was truly there, wide awake. *"Okay, you're losing your mind,"* she whispered to herself.

"Mama, are you busy?" Merci asked Estelle, sensing something unusual, responded,

"No, baby, what's going on? You've been acting a little strange lately," said her mother. "That's to say the least," replied Merci. "I'm feeling very strange lately," she began, struggling to express her recent experiences. "What do you mean?" Estelle inquired. "It's like sometimes I'm not in my body or something," Merci continued. Her words were charged with uncertainty. Her mother was well aware of the situation, but she maintained her facade of ignorance. "What do you mean?" she prodded gently. Merci hesitated at first and then replied, "Oh, it's nothing."

"Oh really?" she said.

Merci finally let it out, "It's just that this morning when I went outside, I saw the city of Nippur. I mean, I really saw it."

Her mother just listened, her face calm as if she had expected this. Merci went on, "I even went into EnLil's temple." Estelle's response was measured, and she replied, "All I can say is maybe it was a mirage, baby." "Really, mama?" she said, feeling overwhelmed, and then she abruptly left the tent, her voice trembling as she cried, *"What's happening to me?"*

Estelle couldn't help but feel guilty. She longed to reveal everything to Merci to ease her mind. But she knew she had to follow the process without deviation.

Chapter 3: Traversing through time

The days and nights seemed to race by; before they knew it, months had passed. And it was time to leave and return to Cambridge. The expedition members were busily packing their equipment. As they smiled and chatted, it was clear that hot showers and proper meals were on everyone's mind. Merci assisted in packing up their tent, but just before leaving, she told Estelle that she wanted one last look at the ruins. Her mother agreed, with the warning to be careful. Merci was off to seize the opportunity.

As she walked towards the temple ruins and along the left side, she noticed there was an opening; it didn't look too deep, so she decided to descend into the darkness. As she descended into the darkness, a sudden Erie draft made her rethink her plan. She grabbed the torch and a box of matches, feeling the weight of unease settling in her chest. She struck the match once, twice, but each time, a strong wind promptly extinguished it. On the 3rd attempt, her trembling hand caused the box of matches to slip from her grip.

Now, she was faced with a dilemma, weighing her options. Should she retreat and return to the surface? Or should she continue downward into the abyss? Determination gripped her, and she chose to press on. The descent into the unknown grew increasingly dark, and Merci's steps became more uncertain. Then, a glimmer of dim light pierces the darkness. It beckoned her forward like a whisper from the depths. Curiosity drove her to place her foot on the next rung of the ladder, but her foot slipped, and she plummeted, her head striking something hard upon landing. No longer conscious, her body lay there lifeless. When she finally regained consciousness, voices filled her ears.

However, the language they spoke was foreign to her, an enigmatic dialect she had never encountered. She struggled to comprehend their words, feeling an unsettling sense of this placement. "Where am I?" she questioned, her voice trembling as she addressed the enigmatic figures surrounding her. Suddenly, a tall, striking man emerged from the crowd, his golden skin mirroring hers. Clad in a warrior's garment, he spoke to her in an unfamiliar tone. Desperate for answers, Merci implored, "Where am I?" With a gentle touch to her forehead, he made it easier for her to understand everything. The suspense thickened as she sought to understand her situation. Setting the stage for a journey into the unknown.

As the shock of the accident begins to wear off, Estelle's world plunges into turmoil. Merci lay unconscious, unresponsive to her mother's desperate pleas. In a frantic rush to the nearest hospital, Estelle clung to hope, anxiously awaiting the doctor's verdict on her daughter's condition. An eternity passes in the waiting room, each moment weighed down by fear and uncertainty.

Finally, Dr. Azizi, the attending physician, approached Estelle with a somber expression addressing her with carefully chosen words, attempting to relay the gravity of the situation. "Hello, Dr. Lowe," he began, "your daughter has sustained a severe head injury from the fall. She appears to have a concussion. We'll need to conduct additional tests to assess the full extent of her injuries, and I promise to keep you informed. Estelle's eyes glistened with anxiety as she inquired, "May I see her, Dr. Azizi?" "Of course," he replied, "But I must warn you that she is still unconscious." Tears still flowed from Estelle's eyes, but she nodded, her need to get to her daughter unwavering. "That's okay," she managed to utter.

What Estelle was not aware of was that, at this very moment, Merci was in a world unlike any she had ever known. An unknown figure in a white robe tended her; he introduced himself as the assistant to Prince Liam, the son of Queen Pue-obe. He explained that she was now in Enlil's temple, the creator of mankind. "Ok," she said, looking around, assessing her situation, struggling to express the inexplicable journey that had brought her to this strange place and time. As she explained, Prince Liam summoned Temple servants to attend to her needs, his eyes locked on to hers with an unsettling familiarity. In her eyes, he glimpsed the spirit of someone he had once known, a maiden from a different time. Thinking out loud, he murmured, "I should never have let you go." At that moment, he was clinging to Merci's hand, with a mixture of love, longing, and appreciation etched across his face. Estelle's thoughts, too, were with her daughter, as she was very worried, hoping that she was not going to lose her.

At that internal moment, Estelle whispered, "Sister, your daughter needs you." But what Estelle was unaware of was that Merci was on a journey of her own. In this mysterious realm, Merci bore an ethereal aura adorned in resplendent garments that were bestowed upon her by her host; it gave her a regal demeanor. Her beautiful, long, raven black hair, typically free-spirited, had been elegantly gathered into a bun, and the fragrance of exotic blossoms permeated the air. In this otherworldly setting, Merci found herself irresistibly drawn to the sense of belonging that enveloped her spirit. Guided as if by unseen hands, Merci was led into a grand chamber, where she was to be presented before the prince and his formidable mother, Queen Pue-obe.

Here, in the presence of royalty and amidst the enigma of this reality, Merci's journey was destined to become even more captivating. "Welcome to the Royal Palace, Merci. I am Queen Pue-obe, and Prince Liam is my son. He told me that you were found in our temple. How did you happen to arrive there?" she asked. Merci looked at her, and she was gloriously wonderful.

 She definitely looked like a queen. "Your majesty," said Merci, "as I told your son, I have no idea how I got here; one moment, I was exploring the tunnel, and the next, honestly, I just don't know, but I do remember falling. Your majesty, can you please tell me where I am?" Queen Pue-Obe's expressions are both gracious and intriguing. "You, my dear, are in the city of Nippur." Merci was astonished. "I can't believe it. I'm actually here."

The Queen's curiosity remained. "Merci, what time have you come from?" the queen asked. Merci replied, "The 21st century, the Year 2007." The Queen's eyes gleamed with interest. "You must tell me everything about your time," she insisted. "Okay," said Merci, realizing that she had an extraordinary opportunity to share her knowledge of the future with this ancient civilization. She began recounting the achievements and, regrettably, the harm mankind had done over the centuries. Little did she know her presence in this ancient world held secrets yet to be unveiled, and her journey had only just begun.

As the sun set over the city, casting a Golden Glow on the ancient buildings, Merci watched the beautiful spectacle; she couldn't help but think of her mother. *Mama would love to be here;* she thought to herself; *she would have so many questions for the queen.* Suddenly, the realization struck her; her mother was probably frantic and worried, searching for her. Merci sighed. She had undoubtedly gotten herself into trouble this time. Turning to her gracious hostess, Merci said, "I must go home. My mother is probably worried and sick about me. How do I return home?" With a soothing tone, the prince reassured her, "Rest now, my child. We will figure that out tomorrow."

As Merci lay down to sleep, her thoughts wandered back to her mother, and in her dream, she could hear her mother crying. "Mama," Merci softly spoke, "leaving one realm, returning to another. Can we go home?" she asked. Estelle, feeling Merci's embrace, responded, "Oh yes, baby." As she held Merci tightly, tears of relief streamed down her cheeks. Merci asked again, "Can we go home?" "As soon as the doctors give the okay, we will go home," her mother reassured her, "I thought I lost you.' "I was only asleep for one day," Merci replied. Estelle corrected her gently, "No! You were unconscious for a whole year." "What day is it?" Merci asked. Estelle informed her that it was the day after Christmas, the year 2008. Merci sighed, "I guessed I missed my birthday." Estelle, overcome with emotion, said, "We have many birthdays to celebrate. The fact that you're alive is the only thing I'm concerned about right now. I love you, Merci; I never want to lose you."

Doctor Azizi entered the room with a knock, "Hello," he greeted them, "How are you feeling today, Merci?" he asked. "I'm feeling like I want to go home." "I understand," said the doctor, "after a couple of more tests, then we'll see." As the doctor exited the room, he asked Estelle to accompany him for a moment. Estelle turned to Merci, "Honey, I'll be right back," as she turned on the television and handed her the remote control.

Watching TV was a treat for Merci because she was generally not allowed to watch it. Estelle often referred to it as an idiot box and firmly believed that it could be detrimental to young minds. She wanted Merci to engage in more meaningful and educational activities, so TV was a restricted pleasure in her household. However, under these circumstances, Merci was given the green light to enjoy some TV to help her pass the time. The colorful screen and variety of programs were like a window into the outside world.

"Yes, doctor Azizi, is there something wrong?" Estelle asked as she stepped out of the room. "Not exactly," said the doctor, "it's just that Merci's blood work has come back, and it seems to have been contaminated somehow."

"What do you mean?"

"I took those samples myself, and I pride myself in being very careful, but it seems that there's some strange substance in her blood, so I must run more tests to make sure that the results I'm getting are correct. I mean, I don't want her to have gotten some kind of infection or disease while she was unconscious in that tunnel," he explained.

"Okay, doctor, but we must leave after the test; I have to get back to Cambridge. Besides, I need to take Merci home. You can always send your results to us in New York or even forward them to her doctor there."

The doctor agreed, and two hours later, they were on their way back to England. Estelle handed in her report on her findings at Nippur, said her goodbyes, and then finally headed back home. After 2 years, Merci would get to see her friends again. She really missed them; she had so much to tell them. On the flight back, Merci wondered why Estelle had not asked her anything about the time she was unconscious; she wished that she would address it. Merci wanted so much to tell her about the experience, but she just didn't ask. It seemed as if she knew something, or she didn't want to know. Merci wasn't sure which one it was.

"Mama, do you believe in God?" asked Merci.

"Well, baby, as a scientist, my beliefs are different from others. I'm trained to deal with actual facts that I know for sure. The concept of God has been debated forever, and no one has ever seen Him that I can talk to. Still, for millions of people, He does exist. I'll tell you one thing for sure: I sure prayed to the All-Powerful to bring you back to me every day while you were unconscious. I do believe that we did not just evolve; somewhere in there, there was intelligent design. Everything did not just suddenly appear and fall into place. We, as archaeologists, are uncovering more and more evidence of that every day. So, the answer to your question is that my spirituality comes from a certain wealth of knowledge, as well as the understanding of oneself and mankind. The older you get, the more insight you'll have; you'll find that you understand so much more about who you are, what role you play, and that Grand design."

"Oh," said Merci.

"So that's why we never go to church, pretty much," said Estelle, and they both started laughing. Pulling up in front of the building was surreal. As they exited the taxi, Estelle reached for her bags. Merci could see that she was struggling. Merci grabbed the bags and took them upstairs; it wasn't that many bags since the bulk of their luggage was being shipped from London. Merci had missed this old building. She was used to the five flights of stairs and was able to get their bags upstairs without her mother's help, but now the shoe was on the other foot because she was worried about her mom; she didn't look so good, maybe she just needed some rest.

Upstairs, as Merci was putting the bags down, Estelle's purse fell, and a prescription bottle rolled out. Bending to pick it up, Merci saw what it was. It was something called captopril. She got a piece of paper, wrote the name down, and quickly returned it to Estelle's purse.

What? Is Mama sick? She would say something to me if she were, or would she?

From then on, Merci kept a close eye on her mother while she did research on the medication that she had just found. Learning that it was an ace inhibitor prescribed for heart conditions.

Chapter 4: Summertime in 2009

Merci and her friends sat on the steps of the building, talking about all the things she saw while she was away; she never revealed the accident that left her unconscious for a year. They updated her on everything she missed. Suddenly, a black SUV pulled in front of the building. Two men got out of the truck and walked towards them. They looked like police or government agents. "Girl, what's going on?" asked Fatima.

"What are they doing here?" said Sariah.

They were identical to each other; they both had black slacks, white shirts, shiny black shoes, and black glasses.

Fatima said, "Guys, they really look like the Men in Black." "Sure," Fatima said, "everybody, you're silly. Men in Black only investigate aliens and stuff. What would they be doing here? Unless, I mean, maybe the crackhead that sleeps on the roof is an alien, yeah, he be beaming it up Scotty all right.

The men walked up the steps, checking each apartment as they went by, stopping on the 4th floor, where they rang Estelle's bell. "Who is it?" she yelled.

The man answered, "Is this the home of Dr. Estelle Lowe?"

"Yes," she said, "how may I help you?" as she opened the door. "Maybe we come in?"

"No, you may not," she answered. Again, she asked, "How may I help you, gentlemen?"

"I'm Agent White, and this is my partner, Agent Jones. Dr. Lowe, we are with Homeland Security, and we have reason to believe that you were present during some shifts in our time space continuum."

"Wait a minute," said Estelle, "First of all, what the hell are you talking about? Time space continuum, remember, gentlemen, you're not talking to a dummy; I'm very aware that that means I was present while someone was time traveling. Is that what you're implying?"

"Yes," that is what I'm saying. The first time was December 12th, 1991, during the excavation of Ur, then again in 1998, and again just recently in 2007, and for us, you are the one constant thing in all three of these events. Let me explain, Dr. Lowe. Your government has developed a program that looks for any temporal anomalies, and the three that we've seen in the past 17 years have happened in places you were visiting. Now, can you explain that, Dr. Lowe?"

"No, sir, I cannot."

"Well, Dr. Lowe, did you notice anything strange, did you see anyone?"

"No sir, not that I can remember."

"Dr. Lowe, was December 12th, 1991, the date your daughter, Merci, was born? We understand that she's adopted. Is that correct?"

"Yes, she is adopted. What does that have to do with anything?" "May I ask how you got the child?"

"I was given a child by a local."

So, do you know anything about this woman?" asked Agent Green.

"No, sir," said Estelle, "I saw her; she gave me the child, and the next minute she was gone."

"That did not seem strange to you," replied the other agent.

"We searched everywhere for her afterward, but we were unable to locate her, so I went through the proper channels and finalized the adoption of the child. Besides, what does my daughter have to do with this?" asked Estelle.

"We aren't quite sure, but believe we're going to find out. Have a good day, Dr. Lowe."

"You too, gentlemen," she said, closing the door behind them. Estelle knew she now had a problem. As Merci walked into the house, she could immediately feel that something was wrong, so she ran directly to her mother's room.

"Mama, are you okay?" she asked.

"Yes, baby, I'm fine, why?" Estelle responded.

"Just checking on you. We saw some strange men dressed in all black coming into the building. We were wondering where they went," said Merci.

"Girl, mind your business, and where's your friends?" asked Estelle.

"Oh yeah, they're going to the movies. I came upstairs to ask if I could go?"

Estelle thought for a moment and said, "I don't know! Who's going, and what movie theater are you going to?"

"Well, Sariah, Sky, Fatima, and we're going to 72nd Street and Broadway.

"Okay," said Estelle, "what time is the movie ending?"

"The show starts at 7:30. I should be home by 10:30 at the latest," said Merci.

"Okay, young lady, call me when the movie is over, so I'll know when to expect you. No boys, Merci!"

"Yes, ma'am!"

"Make sure you come straight home afterward," said her mother.

Merci was 17 years old, yet Estelle was still trying to protect her. She'd be 18 in a matter of months, and she was growing so much so quickly and had grown into quite a beautiful, intelligent young woman. Estelle was very proud.

As the girls settled into their seats at the movie theater, Fatima said, "Girl, did you see the cutie in the second row?"

"Yes, Fatima, I saw him," said Merci, "but he's also with his girlfriend."

"So what? I don't care; it's not like I know her or anything." The reasons are a familiar song, as Merci shook her head in disgust. "Let's go to the pizza shop on Amsterdam Ave," she said.

As the girls crossed Broadway, Merci noticed that a black SUV seemed to be following, but she passed it off as paranoia; they continued down Amsterdam Avenue and into the pizza shop. Ordering a whole pizza, they chose the table next to the window with a great view of the outside. Once again, there was the black SUV. *This is not just paranoia; it appears that this SUV is following us,"* said Merci to herself, and then she started to pay close attention.

Again, as the girls got closer to home, Merci noticed the black SUV, and then suddenly, it dawned on her this was the same SUV that was in front of her building earlier. The windows were dark, so you really couldn't see inside, but she said, "I bet those are the guys that we saw earlier in that truck. Why would they be following us?" she questioned, "Sariah, look over there, do you see that black truck? They seem to be following us."

"Yes, that's right; I noticed it earlier. You have thousands of those things on the road; let's just keep an eye on it."

They continued to walk home together, laughing, talking, and just enjoying the evening; again, they noticed the black SUV had continued to follow once they arrived home. Just as Merci and Fatima started towards the building, the SUV pulled up in front of them, and two men jumped out and walked towards them. They look really scary, and they are definitely the Men in Black. When one of them removed his dark glasses, Merci noticed he didn't have any eyelashes or eyebrows, just piercing black eyes that never blinked.

"Miss Merci Lowe?"

"Yes," said Merci.

"We would like you to come with us."

"What," immediately, she started screaming for her mother, followed by Fatima's screams. Estelle heard all the commotion just as she looked out the window to see the agent grab Merci. "Get your hands off my daughter," she yelled.

As she said that, a few of the guys in front of the park came across the street, heading towards the agents to see exactly what was going on. Soon afterward, Estelle appeared on the street with her phone in hand, "If you do not stay away from us, I'll file harassment charges. Leave us alone." Merci was hysterical as they released her and got into the truck, pulling away.

Merci said, "Mama, what was that all about?"

Immediately, Estelle grabbed her chest and collapsed. Merci hit the stairs running. She ran into the house, got Estelle's bag, and took out the medicines. She rushed back to Estelle's side and quickly placed one of the tiny pills in Estelle's mouth under her tongue. The ambulance arrived and rushed her to the hospital, where she was simultaneously being prepped for surgery. She'd had a massive heart attack. For what felt like an eternity, Estelle was in surgery while Merci anxiously waited for a word about her condition.

Fatima and her grandmother, Miss Fisher, were also present at the hospital. Estelle remained unresponsive, and Merci stayed by her side faithfully. It was heart-wrenching for Merci to see her mother relying on machines to breathe, but she never left her mother's side. Merci talked to her while tenderly washing her face and carefully combed her beautiful long hair every day.

During this trying time, Miss Fisher encouraged Merci to continue with the educational plans she and her mother had made. Merci had important exams coming up, including the high school regions and SATs, and Estelle wouldn't want her to jeopardize her future.

Miss Fisher had been a pillar of support, looking after Merci while Estelle was in the hospital. After diligent preparation, Merci successfully passed both tests with remarkable scores. Fatima, Soraya, and Sky had already taken these exams, setting a high standard for their friend. With Merci's impressive scores, she had the opportunity to choose from any University she desired.

Merci still had previously considered Penn State due to his prestigious archeology program. In August, Merci received her acceptance letter from Penn State, and they were overjoyed that she had chosen their institution. She didn't feel the need to visit the campus because she was already well acquainted with it. Her mother had taught classes there in the past, and she had a colleague who now served as the dean of archeology, so the campus held no surprises for Merci.

Until it was time for Merci to begin school, she continued her daily visits to the hospital to be with her mother. She would read Estelle's favorite magazine, Archeology Digest, and provide her with the care and attention she needed. Brushing her hair, applying lotion to her hands and feet, and attending to her every need became Merci's daily routine.

As the time approached for Merci to begin school, she continued her daily visits to the hospital. One day, Merci took her mother's hand and placed it over her heart. Tears welled up in her eyes, "Mama, please wake up. I need you; you're all I have in this world." She rested her head on her mother's chest, hearing the faint beating of her mother's heart, her tears leaving a salty reminder of the heavy burden she carried.

"Mama, please don't leave me," Merci whispered, leaning forward to kiss her mother's forehead. She was saying a tearful goodbye, uncertain if she'd ever see her alive again. It was time for Merci to leave for school. Leaving the hospital, Merci was troubled by the thought of leaving her mother behind, but she knew she had to complete her education, which was always the top priority for Estelle.

Still, her mother was the most important person in her life, and it was difficult to leave her in the hospital. Merci had the contact information for the doctors and nurses station, ensuring she would stay well informed about her mother's condition. With a heavy heart and tears in her eyes, she boarded the bus bound for Penn State University. Upon arriving at the college, Merci checked in and located her assigned room in a coed dormitory where both male and female students resided.

"I'm going to like it here," Merci remarked to herself as she glanced around. Being the first to arrive in her room, she had first picked the bed and side of the room she wanted to be in. Choosing the nearest bed to the window, she smiled, appreciating the view of the sky and the constant flow of air. About 2 hours later, Merci's roommate, Mary Ellen Baker, from West Virginia, arrived. Mary Ellen had a distinct, charming accent and was quite chatty. Despite the unusual accent, she proved to be a friendly companion.

Once Merci had unpacked and settled into her new surroundings, she decided to take a stroll through the campus. The familiar beauty of the place brought back memories. Over the next couple of months, Merci worked diligently to intergrate herself into college life. Mary Ellen became a close friend, and they spent a lot of time together, studying and discussing the intriguing topic of boys.

Remaining dedicated to her studies, she continued to call the hospital for updates on her mother's condition. The good news was that her mom was no longer reliant on machines to breathe, although she remained unconscious.

This brought great relief to Merci, who eagerly anticipated the winter break so she could return home and share her college experiences with her mother. She missed her dearly and had so much to tell her.

In her college life, Merci was well cared for, with her tuition covered by a trust fund set up by Estelle. This financial support meant she could ask for whatever she needed without any financial concerns. As a child, Merci had never truly considered her status.

Through her travels, she realized that she had more than many of the kids in the country she had visited, but she didn't have the same material possessions as most of the children in her neighborhood. She wore secondhand clothes and received only one pair of sneakers and one pair of shoes every year. Yet, Merci was beginning to experience a newfound sense of independence.

Thinking back, Merci realized that she never really noticed if Estelle was rich or poor; it just seemed that her mother always provided whatever she needed. Estelle has been saving for Merci to attend college, and her financial advisor had suggested that Merci take a driving class to get a license. It would be more convenient, especially given her frequent travels back and forth to New York.

Merci decided to purchase a gold Honda Accord, and she had her driver's license for just a week when the dorm mate called her on the phone. Restless, she asked who it was. His response was, "It's the hospital." Rushing to the phone, fearing for her mother. She answered, and Nurse Patel spoke to her.

Merci's heart raced when she heard the news her mother had regained consciousness. She couldn't contain her joy and said, "Thank you, Most High!" She also thanked Nurse Patel, who assured her that it was a pleasure to share the good news. Inquiring if she could speak to her mother, she was informed that Estelle was currently undergoing a test. However, the nurse provided her with the room number and suggested that Merci call her back in a few hours.

Merci searched for a pen, puzzled by the lack of writing instruments in a college. Frustrated, she decided to rely on her memory but then quickly changed her mind. She declared hell with that and rushed home to pack her things. Excitement and anxiety filled the air. Merci shouted three words: Mama is awake! Mary Ellen, her roommate, ran to the window and told her to make sure to call her when she arrived. Without wasting any time, Merci jumped into her little gold car and headed home down I-95 North.

Taking less than 3 hours, Merci arrived at Columbia Presbyterian Hospital. She parked her car and made her way into the hospital, stopping at the gift shop to purchase flowers and balloons for her mom.

As she left the gift shop, the evening security guard, Mark, went over and stuck up the conversation. He asked how she'd been and mentioned that it had been a while since they'd seen each other. Merci acknowledged the time that had passed and continued her way to the elevator. Mark mentioned that he had heard Dr. Lowe's recovery and suggested that he might see Merci again the next day. Merci replied, "I really should have been here when she woke up. Well, have a great day, Mark," as she stepped into the elevator.

Everyone at the hospital was pleasantly surprised to see Merci, and before visiting her mother, she had a conversation with her doctor. The doctor explained that Estelle's sudden recovery was nothing short of a miracle but cautioned that she was not entirely out of danger. Merci showed them that she understood and expressed her gratitude for the exceptional care they have provided for her mother.

Upon entering her mother's hospital room, Merci was greeted by an array of flowers and cards from Estelle's colleagues and students. And when Estelle caught sight of Merci, her face lit up with a smile.

"There's my beautiful college student," she exclaimed.

Merci ran to her mother's side, "Mama, I love you so much. Are you okay?"

"Yes, baby, the doctor said I'm doing fine."

"So, when can I take you home?" Merci asked.

"Tomorrow," Estelle replied, "I'm being discharged tomorrow."

They talked for a while, and then Merci went home to prepare for her mother's return. She assured the doctor that her mother would follow all his instructions, making her recovery as comfortable as possible. She took charge of preparing Estelle's meals whenever Miss Fisher didn't, and together, they made sure that Estelle didn't exert any extra stress on her heart. Even though tomorrow was Merci's birthday, it wasn't a significant concern at the time. Her top priority was getting her mother back to full health.

As the winter vacation passed, Merci contemplated transferring from Penn State to be closer to her mother, but her mother firmly opposed the idea. Insisting that Merci continue her studies at Penn State to accommodate this decision, Merci arranged for 24-hour home care for her mother to ensure someone was always there to look after her.

On January 12th, Merci returned to Penn State. She made it a point to speak with her mother every morning before the first class and every night before bed. This was her second semester, and the workflow was more challenging but manageable for her. Much of the material was familiar to her due to her experience in various excavations during her youth. She found herself ahead of her classmates by a considerable margin.

However, on the evening of January 22nd, 2010, Merci called her mother and received no answer. This worried her, as Estelle's home attendant would typically call Merci's cell if anything was amidst. Merci made the call again, growing increasingly anxious when there was no answer. She tried calling the home attendance cell phone, but that, too, went unanswered. Frustration and worry mounting, Merci attempted a few more times before finally giving up and going to sleep. That night, Merci had a haunting dream. She found herself in a long, dark tunnel with a brilliant light at its end. As she approached the light, her mother emerged, clad in a pristine white gown, and she smiled at her. Her mother spoke softly, telling Merci that she was no longer of the Earth; she referred to Merci as the light of the world and said, "You are ready, my child." Confused, Merci asked, "Ready for what, mama?" as Estelle faded away.

Awakened the next morning, Merci's heart was heavy. She attempted to call Estelle once more, desperately hoping to hear her voice. Just then, she heard the dorm mother's voice calling her name. Merci Lowe, you're wanted in the Dean's office. As she sat outside the Dean's office, her mind raced with worry. She couldn't understand why she was summoned. Her thoughts were interrupted when Mr. Wineglass, the dean, appeared in the doorway, inviting her inside.

In a somber expression, he began, "Hello, Ms. Lowe, I called you into my office with some unfortunate news. Your mother, Dr. Estelle Lowe, passed away yesterday from a massive heart attack. Our deepest condolences to you. At that moment, Merci registered nothing of the rest of what he said. The only thought that echoed in her mind was the painful realization that she had just lost the only family she had ever known.

Leaving the Dean's office, Merci's legs felt like they might give way, and her vision grew increasingly blurry. The journey back home felt like it took forever, now carrying the weight of unbearable sorrow, and her world had been turned upside down. With uncontrollable tears streaming down her cheeks, she thought she had just returned to school after having a joy-filled holiday with her mother. They had made wonderful memories together, and the thought of life without her mother had never crossed her mind.

Now, she faced the daunting question of how to continue her education when all she could do was grieve. *Who would love her now,* she thought, *without her mother by her side?*

Estelle Aristarr Lowe left this world on January 22nd, 2010; she had prepared for her daughter's future. Her will was being handled by her attorney, and she left Merci a heartfelt letter, which read, "My darling daughter, if you're reading this letter, I have left my earthly body and transferred into a heavenly one. I am fine, and I know this will be a very difficult time for you. You, my love, have made this life worth living and brought me so much joy and happiness. Thank you for that. My love will continue to watch over you forever. I love you, Merci.

Soon, all will be revealed to you. Financially, you are set for life. I have made sure of that. My love, stay strong, and most of all, remember everything I taught you. For soon, it will all make sense. I asked only one thing: please do not allow them to embalm me; keep my body intact. Goodbye, baby, until we meet again. Your mama!"

While at the grave site, Merci noticed the black SUV, but being preoccupied with her grief, she excused it. What she didn't realize was they were not there for her mother; they were there for her. The funeral and the days that followed passed quickly. Merci said goodbye to her friends and returned to Penn State. Merci cherished her time at the University.

She had always been fascinated by all things ancient and old ever since she had accompanied her mother on her first archaeological dig to the Valley of Kings in Egypt when she was just 7 years old. This experience had left a lasting impact on her, and this was why she chose archeology as her major. It gave her an escape and allowed her to pursue something that she truly loved while keeping her close to her mother.

It seemed that summer vacation was taking forever to arrive. Just before vacation started, Merci received a letter from an attorney she recognized as the one who had handled Estelle's personal affairs. Her heart filled with mixed emotions, and she opened the letter with instructions: "Please go to the Bank of New York on 57th Street and 2nd Avenue. Ask for the bank president, Mr. Levy. Provide him with your identification, and he will give you all the details of account number 34-751-5-10901. Good luck, Miss Lowe. Sincerely, RJ Branch attorney at law." Tears welled up in Merci's eyes.

It had only been a few months since her mother's passing, and the pain of the loss was still very raw. Pulling up in front of the familiar five story building, Merci couldn't help but feel an intense mix of emotions. This was her childhood home, the one she had shared with her mother, yet she couldn't shake the feeling that there was more out there for her, something beyond these familiar walls.

As she reflected, she heard a scream from the window, "Hey, girl, welcome home!" Merci couldn't help but feel that her journey had only just begun. Spotting her best friend, Fatima Fisher, hanging out the fourth floor window, she asked, "Do you plan on helping me upstairs?" Merci and Fatima had shared a deep friendship since their early childhood, a bond that had always felt more like sisterhood than friendship. Their connection had a unique origin. Fatima's grandmother and Estelle have been neighbors and found themselves raising little girls within 6 months of each other. Mrs. Fisher, Fatima's grandmother, provided childcare services to the neighborhood, offering to board children for a fee.

This arrangement meant they would often have different kids living with her 7 days a week, and when Fatima's mother passed away, her grandmother, Miss Fisher, took her in. The two women, Estelle and Ms. Fisher, formed an unlikely but strong friendship. A world-traveled archaeologist and Fisher, who had never left the neighborhood, found common ground in their love for the two girls. Whenever Dr. Lowe left on one of her archaeological expeditions when Merci was just a baby, Miss Fisher would care for her. Now, with both women gone, the girls were left to navigate the world on their own.

As Merci climbed the stairs to the 4th floor, Fatima eagerly waited at the top, embracing her with a tight hug and nearly squeezing her breathless.

"Girl, I miss you so much. Things around me just ain't been the same without you," Fatima explained.

Merci tried to downplay it, saying, "It looks like the same old neighborhood to me, Fatima," and they both burst into laughter. Curiously, Fatima asked about Adonis, "So where is the Don? Did he know you were coming home today?" Merci replied, "No, I wanted to surprise him." Fatima suggested, "Well, let me throw something on, and we'll go find him." Merci agreed and added, "I'm going next door to unpack. Knock when you are ready, Miss, I'll take forever."

They both share a light-hearted moment; the familiarity of their friendship made Merci feel right at home. As Merci stepped back into the hallway, the aroma of collard greens and cornbread smacked her dead in the face. *Wow, it's been months since I had a real home-cooked meal,* she thought, but today, she didn't have time for that.

She placed her key in the door and slowly opened it. At any moment, she expected to hear her mama, but the realization that she was gone was evidence of the eerie quietness that followed. The house had a stale smell, but after all, it had been closed for 4 months. She walked into her bedroom, and nothing had changed; it still looked the way it looked when she left to go away to school, but it felt different and empty like she sometimes felt.

Deciding to take a quick shower, she walked into the bathroom. There was a knock at the door, "damn, Fatima, that was the fastest you've ever got dressed," she snatched open the door. And there he stood, the love of her life, "Hey baby, why didn't you call me?" She ran straight into his arms, the bathrobe flying open and all. She didn't care; Adonis was all that she needed.

Looking deep into her big, beautiful eyes as if searching for her soul, without resisting her waiting lips, gave him the okay to continue. She was aroused and felt this heat that she had never felt before. What she was feeling now was so intense, and she wanted nothing more; no, she needed relief. The closer Adonis got to her, the louder Mama's voice got in her head, but at this point, there was no turning back; she closed her eyes and surrendered to the powerful attraction between them.

Closing the door behind her, they made love until the early hours of the morning, their passion consuming them, and afterward, they fell asleep in each other's arms. They had been together throughout high school, and they had plans to eventually marry. However, Adonis was fully aware that Merci's career as an archaeologist was her primary focus. Besides, her mother never really approved of him, strongly believing that he wasn't the right match for her. Estelle made her disapproval clear every time she saw them together. But their love was undeniable; it was evident to anyone who knew them.

A crack in the window allowed a gentle spring breeze into the room. The scent of the awakening season filled the air, and the off-white sheer curtains billowed in the wind as if dancing in the morning light. As the curtain suede gently from side to side, the morning sun tenderly kissed Adonis' handsome face as Merci lay beside him, contemplating their true future together. She pondered what kind of life they could have, especially with her unwavering commitment to archeology. She wasn't sure that he understood her priorities.

Oh! How she loved him, she thought to herself as she lay there, watching him sleep. Again, asking what kind of life could they have? He never really wanted to leave the neighborhood, but she was going to see the world. Laying there next to Adonis, she couldn't help but feel conflict. She knew that she loved him with all her heart, but her dreams of becoming an archaeologist were pulling her in a different direction, and she knew that her career would take her far from the neighborhood where they had both grown up.

Adonis had always been content with staying put; it was a source of tension between them, but still, they tried not to let it get in their way. Merci knew that she couldn't give up on her dreams; she wanted to see the world and uncover its secrets, and she couldn't let anything stand in her way, but she also knew that Adonis would always have a special place in her heart no matter where life took her.

Merci decided to share the information in the letter from her mother with Adonis. She was going to the bank today as the letter had instructed, so she asked him to come with her. As they made their way to the bank, Adonis held her hand all the way, providing a sense of security. They were there to meet Mr. Levi, the bank president, as per the instructions in Dr. Lowe's letter. As they walked into the bank, Merci couldn't help but notice how Grand and all the building was. The ceiling was high and Dome-like. They couldn't help but admire it. It was very impressive, with an air of luxury and importance.

Mr. Levi, an elderly gentleman, approached them slowly and greeted them warmly, "Hello, I'm Mr. Levi. How may I assist you?" Merci introduced herself and explained the reason for her visit, handing over the letter from Dr. Lowe's attorney. Mr. Levi read the letter carefully and then looked at them with a serious expression. "I see," he said, "Well, this is quite unusual, but I think I can help you; follow me, please." Merci looked back at Adonis, indicating that he should come along.

Mr. Levi led them to his office to discuss the matter further. Merci gave Mr. Levi the account number 34-751-635 10901. He then placed some papers in front of her, asking her for her identification. He began to explain the account to her. Her mother had left strict instructions that she was to be given $100,000. This money was to go towards her education, and upon her 21st birthday, she would receive another $150,000. "What?" she said, "Did I hear that correctly, $250,000?" Merci was ecstatic. "I had no idea that Mama had that kind of money," and to think her younger years were spent in clothes that came from Goodwill often made her the subject of bullies' constant jokes, but who's laughing now? She thought.

Merci had the bank transfer $70,000 to Penn State and the remainder put into an account in her and Adonis' name. Filled with gratitude, she thanked Mr. Levi. As she left the building, a sense of real curiosity filled her. She needed to know more about her mother, the esteemed Dr. Lowe.

Once they returned to the car, Adonis asked if she was hungry, nodding yes and rubbing her stomach. Merci suggested a little place on the Upper East Side named 'duBignons, which was known for its authentic Cajun cuisine. Adonis parked the car in the garage, and they walked over to the restaurant. The exterior was inviting, and the exciting customers were satisfied. You could tell by the smiles on their faces.

Once inside, the soft music and the soft whispers of its guests created a romantic atmosphere. The hostess seated them at a quiet table in the corner as if she knew they wanted to be alone. As they settled into their seats, the dancing light of the candle on the table caught Merci's attention, setting the mood for a wonderful evening. As they indulged in The Delectable Southern Cuisine, the air was filled with a sense of romance and intimacy. The soft glow of the candlelight illuminated Merci's face, making her look even more stunning than before. Adonis couldn't help but admire her beauty and charm, feeling grateful to have her by his side.

However, as she reached over to take a piece of chicken from his plate, Adonis couldn't resist teasing her about her appetite, "Don't you have your own food, girl? You are looking a little wide around the hips," he joked, but the truth was, he loved every curve of her body, and the thought of ever losing her was unthinkable.

Despite the distance between them due to her schooling in Pennsylvania, Adonis was determined to keep their love strong. He knew that He could have any girl he wanted, but Merci was worth waiting for; after all, true love is worth the sacrifice.

Chapter 5: Anu

Anu was furious. He was now sure that there was a Royal heir unknown to him. Not yet knowing where she was, but he was aware that he must find her soon. She would soon be too powerful to control. He told his Royal minister of state to recall the Royal House; this meant every Royal male and female must give an account to him immediately. After explaining the Task to the Sebittu and the Hallaku, he dispatched them to all corners of the universe. He wanted this child found and extinguished, and He was willing to destroy all he had created to find her. Had he been so into his human creation that his house was now in shambles?

They came from all Realms of the universe. The Royal house was now in chaos; you could hear the whispers all through the Great Hall. "Why did Anu call them all here?" One by one, he questioned them telepathically entering each Celestial being, and he found no deception in them; they knew nothing of this child. The king was infuriated by this; the child did exist, yet there had been no known new births in the Royal line for thousands of years, so he decided to take matters into his own hands and use his power to find her. He began to scour the universe, searching every corner and every realm, looking for any trace of this child. He searched for years, using his immense power to peer into every corner of the universe, but still, he found nothing.

As time passed, Anu was quite confused and growing weary of his search, realizing that she may be hiding in a realm beyond his reach, which was impossible, or perhaps she was being protected by powerful beings he didn't know of as of yet. The feeling of defeat overtook him, but he could not give up. The thought of her growing up to become a powerful ruler with the potential to overthrow him was too great a risk.

Continuing his search for years, the Anasari of the second house of the Fallen and the Lammasu of the fifth house reminded the king of the prophecy that states a child would be born of the Royal House of the Annunaki. As they reminded him of the prophecy, these words came to him. Of the seven, one shall come, able to undo all the seven have done, of the royal house, she shall be, and she shall rule through eternity." *"This can't be,"* he thought out loud; this prophecy was foretold many millennia ago.

It was imperative that she be found; if not, she can end his Reign. Anu was King of the Gods, The God of the heavens, lord of the constellation, and he ruled over spirits and demons.

Anu was the God of the sky, and with his sons, Enlil, god of the air, and Enki, god of the water, they formed the Heavenly Triad. Anu asked Lliabrat, his assistant, "Had a message been sent to the queen?" He noticed that neither she nor her sister, Ishtar, had yet arrived. Lliabrat informed the king that the queen was in her chamber and would soon present herself to the court for questioning. Where is Ishtar, and why has she not answered my call? Just as he asked, the goddess Ishtar appeared. "My king, why have you summoned me?" she asked, and then she took her seat among the goddesses in court.

Anu began to speak, "A royal heir has been conceived, and I am not aware of any new births in the Royal Line. Would you have any idea of how this happened?" he said as he attempted to enter her Celestial body for telepathic questioning, she stopped him, "how dare you ask me such a thing?" she said as she rose from her seat. The idea had always been that only a royal female's birth could add a strand to the Royal DNA column.

The king was puzzled by Ishtar's defiance. He had never encountered such behavior from her before. Shocked by her reaction. Anu had always been able to use his abilities to communicate with the goddesses, but Ishtar's reaction was unexpected and suspicious. "I apologize, my lady," he said, attempting to calm her down, "Ishtar, this is of great importance to the fate of this kingdom. We must find this child and ensure she does not pose a threat to this realm." The king knew that a child was born of the Royal House of the Annunaki; this prophecy says the child would come to undo all the seven had done.

Knowing that Ishtar's reaction was suspicious, Anu couldn't afford to lose his temper; he had to find the child and eliminate the threat she posed, no matter what the cost. The future of the Gods and the universe hung in the balance. Ishtar's mind raced as she left the Great Hall; she knew the consequences. If Anu discovered her sister's transgression, it would be catastrophic. Ishtar was determined to protect her sister and the child, but how could she do it? The king was all-powerful, and he had already dispatched his most trusted emissary to search for the child. Ishtar knew that she had to act quickly as she departed for her sister's Chambers. Ishtar's mind was racing with ideas of how they could protect the child and keep her hidden from the king's reach. She needed a plan, a way to outmaneuver the powerful God and keep the child safe.

The tension was palpable as she weighed her options. Anu's power was unmatched, but Ishtar was determined to protect her sister and the child. She had to act quickly and decisively. Ishtar knew that if Anu found out that Antu had mixed blood with the humans, she and her child would be annihilated. She knew that they must protect this child at all costs. Although this was all Anu's doing, he had been spending so much time with his human creation that Antu felt that he loved this mankind more than her, and she wanted to see for herself why they were so special to him.

The king had many consorts; it was permitted for the males of their species to lay with the daughters of men, but it was forbidden for the females of the royal house to lay with human males because the Royal Line is continued by the female and if a royal female were to procreate with a human male not only would the Royal Line be contaminated, but this would create the ultimate Hybrid human with untold, unknown powers.

Merci had already been born when Antu realized the gravity of her choice. She had laid with the human male, and the birth was the product of this forbidden union. Antu knew that if Anu found out both, she and Merci would be killed, so she made the difficult decision to hide Merci away, far from the prying eyes of the Annunaki for years; she kept Merci hidden, doing everything in her power to keep her safe. But now, with Anu on the hunt for the missing Royal heir, her worst fears were starting to come true. Merci was now an adult, and Antu knew that she couldn't keep her hidden forever; she had to find a way to protect her from Anu's Wrath. Not exactly sure how, as she paced back and forth in her chambers, she couldn't help but feel a sense of hopelessness wash over her.

Suddenly, there was a knock at the door. The queen froze, her heart pounding in her chest, knowing she had to be careful, that even the slightest mistake would lead to her and her daughter's demise. "Who is it?" she asked, trying to keep her voice steady. "Ishtar," came the reply from the other side of the door. She breathed a sigh of relief. Her sister was the only Annunaki who knew about Merci's existence and had promised to keep her safe.

The queen quickly opened the door, letting her sister inside, feeling a knot in her stomach. "Anu is getting closer," Ishtar said, her voice low and urgent, "We have to move Merci, and we have to do it now." When Merci was born, Antu disguised herself and appeared in the faraway future at one of her sister's digs on Earth, leaving her daughter with Estelle Lowe/ Ishtar, the world-famous archaeologist. The only way to protect Merci was to hide her, entrusting Merci to Estelle.

When Merci turned seven years old, Antu revealed herself to her sister and instructed her to keep the child hidden from everyone, including the other gods. Antu hoped with time, the king's rage would subside, and he would forget about the child altogether, but after years, the queen realized that the king's obsession with finding the child had only grown stronger, knowing it was only a matter of time before he would uncover the truth and that Merci would be in grave danger. She had to come up with a plan, and fast she called upon her sisters, Ishtar and Ninhursag, and together they decided that the best course of action was to send Merci away to a distant Galaxy, where she would be far away from the king's reach, but where was that?

As Merci grew up, she never knew anything about her biological parents, and she never really questioned it; she knew only that she was adopted by Estelle, a very famous archeologist and a kind and loving woman who always had her best interests at heart. Merci now knew that there was more to her story than what she was told.

Antu was the Annunaki Queen. She had three sons, Enlil, Enki, and Sin, and three daughters, Ninlil, Ninki, and Ningal. Her sisters were Ishtar and Ninhursag; they were among 50 Royals who were in charge of the 600 lower gods of the Annunaki that had come to Earth. Antu's servant girl knocked before entering her chambers with her head bowed. She informed Antu that the king requested her presence in the Great Hall immediately. Antu knew at once what this was about, and she feared for her well-being.

If Anu ever knew of her indiscretion, she would be cast into Oblivion and her daughter with her. Antu's first thought was to run fast and far, but she realized that would not save her daughter. It was very hard to tell anything but the truth to the king once he entered the celestial body because the inner being could not lie.

Queen Antu was the highest-ranking female of the Annunaki Nordics, as well as their lead scientist. She and her siblings were responsible for the creation of humanity, but now she had a secret that could bring down her kingdom. She knew she had to face Anu and answer his questions truthfully. As she made her way to the Great Hall, she could feel the tension in the air; all the Annunaki had been summoned, and she knew it had to do with her daughter.

The queen entered The Great Hall. Her beauty was unmatched; all in attendance rose to their feet, and there was a sudden stillness and silence as all beings in attendance showed their reverence for their queen. Anu watched as his Queen took charge of her audience. He, as well as everyone else, was in awe of her. Antu was in control of the room before the king could ask her any questions.

The Queen began to speak. Standing tall and Regal, commanding attention with every word she spoke. "My king," she began, "I remind you that we cannot act recklessly in the search for this child; we must consider all possibilities and gather all information before making any rash decisions. This child may be the key to our future and the future of our kingdom. We can't afford to lose her. The king nodded in agreement, recognizing the wisdom in the Queen's words.

"You're correct, Antu," said the king. "We must be cautious," the queen continued, "I suggest we gather all available resources and information both from our records and those of the humans. We must also consider the possibility that this child may not even be on earth but in another realm or dimension." Anu was impressed by the queen's strategic thinking. Leaning forward on his throne, Anu couldn't help but feel a sense of suspicion lingering in the air.

Why was Antu speaking with such authority, passion, and confidence? He wondered, his eyes narrowing as he listened to the Queen's words; there was something in her tone that made him uneasy. *Was she hiding something from him?* Anu and Antu had been together for thousands of years, but now he couldn't shake the feeling that she was keeping secrets from him.

"Your words are wise, my queen," Anu said, trying to keep his tone neutral, "I am sure there's something you're not telling us. Do you know something about this child that you're not sharing?" Antu's expression remained stoic as she replied, "My king, I assure you that I have no knowledge of this child. However, as the lead scientist of the Annunaki, I am willing to dedicate all my resources to finding her." Anu nodded slowly, but his suspicion remained. Anu was not able to shake off the feeling that there was more to this than the queen was letting on. Anu made a mental note to keep a close eye on her and all of her actions. If there was a conspiracy afloat, he wouldn't let it go unchecked. She had bought herself some time now; hopefully, she could find a way to protect Merci and her Secret.

Breathing a sigh of relief as the audience was dismissed. Yes, she had bought some time, but the fear of the king finding out the truth still lingered. Needing to act fast to protect Merci back in her chambers, she thought of a plan. She had to reach out again to Ishtar and seek help. Her sister had always been known for her cunning and resourcefulness, and the queen trusted her completely. Yet reaching Ishtar wasn't that easy. Antu summoned her servant girl and asked her to again send for Ishtar; she knew that time was of the essence, and she needed to act fast.

Antu sat down together with her thoughts and planned her next move. Knowing the road ahead would not be easy, but she was determined to protect her daughter at all costs.

Chapter 6: Saying Good-bye

Merci began the daunting task of going through Estelle's things, her senses heightened by the strong scent of Jean Nate filling the room. She looked around as if in a daze and had to leave for a minute to compose herself, promising not to get emotional. She just wanted to get through it, knowing it was not going to be easy. Adonis was in the living room watching sports when he noticed Merci leaning against the wall opposite Estelle's room.

Rising from the couch, unsure if he should approach her, he still walked over and put his arms around her. They stood there for a moment, holding each other tightly without saying a word. At this point, Adonis knew that Merci just needed somebody to lean on, a shoulder to cry on, and he was there to support her through this time.

Once Merci returned to Estelle's room, Adonis stayed with her, giving her the support she needed to finish sorting and packing Estelle's belongings. They worked for hours, and Merci put all of her mother's papers and research on and around her desk; she would go through them later. By the end of the evening, they were both exhausted, and Merci ordered food from Sylvia's Soul Food restaurant before they went to bed. Still, sleep was elusive for Merci, who was tossing and turning all night.

Finally getting out of the bed, not wanting to disturb Adonis, she tiptoed around the apartment, taking in all the memories and weight of her loss. Knowing that this was only the beginning of her grieving process, she would need to find a way to say goodbye to her mother in her own time and in her own way. Sitting behind her mother's desk brought back the fact that she was alone; she was lost without her.

Looking around the room, she saw pictures of herself and Estelle reminiscent of a time when they had each other; now she was gone. Merci wondered why there were no pictures of Estelle's family anywhere. From what Merci remembered, Estelle never spoke of her family, where they were from, or where they were, or even where she was from.

Estelle always responds to Merci's questions about them with a vague answer. She would say that they had died when she was young and that she didn't remember them. All of Estelle's personal papers had been removed upon her death by her attorney. Merci wondered why and made a mental note to ask Estelle's attorney for access to them;

maybe she could find a birth certificate or something to give her some idea of who Estelle Aristarr Lowe was.

Merci continued to make her way through the tons of papers, hoping to understand them better. Before she knew it, the morning light was creeping through the window. Getting up to refresh her tea, she noticed several boxes in the closet labeled Sumerians one through twenty; this was Estelle's life work, and Merci wanted to continue it. *"What better time than now,"* she thought.

As she began to sift through the boxes, she realized just how much work her mother had put into studying the Sumerians. She had always known that Estelle was a dedicated researcher, but seeing the vast amount of information and notes that her mother had accumulated over the years was overwhelming. Despite feeling daunted, Merci was determined to continue her mother's work. Spending the next several days pouring over the contents of these boxes, trying to make sense of the complex theories and concepts her mom had spent her life researching.

As she delved deeper into the research, she couldn't help but feel a sense of all her mother's passion and dedication. She had always known that Estelle was a brilliant scholar, but seeing her work up close was truly eye-opening. Days passed, and Merci began to feel a sense of purpose, a sense of direction, knowing Estelle's Legacy was too important to let go to waste. Merci was determined to carry on her work; she started making plans to continue researching the Sumerians, and she even reached out to some of her mother's former colleagues for guidance and support despite her sadness and loss.

Her mother, heavy in her heart, Merci was slowly starting to find a new sense of hope and purpose; she knew that her mom would have been proud of her carrying on her life's work, and that thought brought a smile and a small measure of comfort to Merci. Box after box, she read and could clearly see that it was all very, very interesting, but it was not just the Sumerian but also the Royal family of the Annunaki.

The Sumerians believed these were the gods of the heavens; they called them sky gods; none of this was new to Merci because, as a little girl, she read books on the subject, and this was something straight out of Chariot of the Gods.

Opening new boxes, she found some of them were filled with pictures of ancient ruins, some had symbols, and each picture explained its place of discovery and its origin. Two pictures particularly stood out, one a golden wing disc encrusted with emeralds, rubies, and diamonds; it was unlike anything Merci had ever seen, but this one was not labeled like the others; it just said Annunaki Royal seal. The other picture had writing on it.

Merci began to translate the story that unfolded; it spoke of a prophecy the Sumerians believed about the return of the Gods, and it also spoke of a war between the Annunaki tribes. One tribe belonged to Enki, and the other Enlil. They were brothers, and they fought over the Earth. One wanted to destroy mankind, and the other wanted to save it. The prophecy also spoke of the birth of a child of royal blood, a gift to humanity. This child would be part human and part god with the power to save or destroy mankind.

Continuing to dig through the boxes, Merci was in shock as she read the words, wondering what they all meant. She continued to pour over the material and couldn't help but feel a deep sense of connection to her mother's work; it was as if Estelle was still guiding her even after death, urging her to uncover the secrets of the ancient world and discover the truth behind this prophecy. *"Wow,"* Merci thought, "what a story," but the question in her mind was, "Why was Estelle so interested in this prophecy?" The more she read, the more she wanted to know. Hearing Adonis moving around in the bathroom, she hollered, "Morning honey."

As he made his way down the hall, he kissed her and said, "You didn't sleep much last night, huh?"

 "No," she replied, "I got up. I didn't want to disturb you. Are you hungry?"

"Yeah, what's for breakfast?" he said.

The summer that they spent together brought them closer. He told her of his dreams of owning his own record label; he said he wanted it to be bigger than Bad Boy Records. Merci said, "Well, first, you need to find yourself a biggie." They both burst out laughing, but Adonis was very serious; they spent a lot of time talking. She would soon return to school to finish her Masters. They planned on getting married once she graduated. He agreed to wait because Merci definitely wanted children with him but remembered living from excavation to excavation with her mother, and she didn't really want that for her children, although it was an awesome experience.

Merci was lost deep in thought about the future when Adonis interrupted her, "What are you thinking about, beautiful?" She smiled at him and replied, "Just thinking about the future, our future, it's exciting and scary all at the same time." Adonis took her hand and squeezed it gently, "I know what you mean, but we'll face it together. Whatever the future holds, we will be there for each other." Merci smiled again and leaned in to kiss him, "I love you." "I love you, too," he replied.

As they ate breakfast, she told him about the discovery of her mother's interest in the Sumerians and the prophecy that Estelle had uncovered. Intrigued by this, they spent the morning going through the boxes together; the more they read, the more fascinated they became. Merci was determined to find out more about her mother and her interest in this prophecy. She contacted Estelle's attorney to access her mother's personal papers.

Summer came to an end, and Merci prepared to return to school. She and Adonis talked about their plans as they said goodbye; she couldn't help but feel a ping of sadness, knowing she would miss him terribly. She knew that they would stay in touch and that their love would endure, she hoped. Merci boarded the plane and settled in her seat, thinking about the summer she had spent with him and the discoveries she had made about her mom's life's work. She knew that the future had many challenges and uncertainties, but she was ready to face them head-on as long as he was by her side.

After returning to school, Merci found herself buried in books and research, but her mind often wondered about the mysterious Sumerian prophecy and her mother's fascination with it. She longed to learn more and understand why it had captivated Estelle so much. So, in her spare time, she pulled out her mother's notes and artifacts, trying to piece together the story of the Anunnaki and their supposed return to Earth. The more she read, the more she felt a sense of urgency, as if time was running out.

Meanwhile, Adonis was busy pursuing his dreams of starting his own record label; he poured his heart and soul into finding new talent and producing music that would make an impact in the industry. He often wished that she could be there with him to share in his success and celebrate their achievements together, but despite the distance between them, they made time for each other, often staying up late into the night on video calls, sharing their dreams and aspirations. Adonis knew that Merci's career was important to her, but he also wanted to show her that he could take care of her and their future family.

The time back at school seems shorter than usual. Maybe it was that Fort Apache mixtape pumping in her ears daily. She likes this group, and if Adonis could sign them, it would be an asset to the company he was creating. It felt great passing the dorms every day because living there had been hectic, and Merci needed her privacy. Living in a private residence gave her that feeling of home that she missed so much. Merci and her roommate, Mary Ellen, had rented a nice little house in a quiet neighborhood not far from campus. There was a frat house on the corner, but they really weren't a problem.

After a long day of classes and research, Merci pulled into the driveway and saw Mary Ellen and her boyfriend; they waved. She smiled, parked her car, and took her stuff into the house. Mary Ellen was Merci's college roommate. They had shared a dorm room, but this house was nice and cozy. The living room was large and inviting, and the big screen TV that hung on the wall made it more inviting. This was her temporary home, and it served its purpose. She was actually glad that she only had 2 years left to earn her master's, hoping it would go quickly.

Once Merci got settled, she attempted to reach Adonis, but there was no answer, so she left him a message and hung up. After a shower and a sandwich, she fell asleep. Most of Merci's spare time in college was spent doing research on her mother and her mother's research into the Anunnaki. The Anunnaki and the ancient Sumerians were fascinating subjects; she had always been interested in mythology and history.

One day, she put Estelle's name in a search engine and was very surprised at what she found. She knew that her mother was a world-renowned expert in the field of ancient Sumerian culture and mythology, and Merci admired her mother's passion for the subject. As she read more about Estelle, she came across a photo of a dig. This dig was excavated during the 1800s. There was a picture of all the archaeologists involved in the excavation, and Estelle Lowe was standing in the third row in the middle. Merci did a double take; she looked for the names of all of the archaeologists underneath the picture just to make sure that it was her mother. She looked for her name, and there it was. How was this at all possible? Her mother was not over 50 when she passed, so why was there a picture here of her from August 1843; none of this made any sense.

Chapter 7: Adonis

As the summer sun rose in the sky, Merci longed for some relief from the stifling heat. She and her friends, Fatima and Sariah, were eager to find something to do to pass the time now that school was out. Merci was rummaging through her closet for a suitable outfit and settled on a flowery sundress, hoping it would provide some relief from the oppressive weather.

As she was getting dressed, her mother called out to her from the other room, interrupting her thoughts. "I'm coming," said Merci as she went to see what her mother needed, only to be handed a ticket for the cleaners and instructed to pick up the living room curtains. She was also given some extra cash to treat herself and her friends to some ice cream, a small consolation for the mundane errand.

As Merci and her friends made their way down the steps of their rundown building, they encountered Miss Fisher, Fatima's grandmother, who was in the middle of scolding her wayward granddaughter yet again. Merci couldn't help but feel a twinge of guilt, wondering when some of her good habits would rub off on her friend.

Despite the building's condition and the unpleasant odor that seemed to permeate every floor, the girls continued on their way, eager to escape their surroundings. She ain't nothing but a gold digger was blaring from the Boombox in front of the park, and Sariah was sitting on the bench listening to her brother and a group of his friends spit Kanye's verses; the air was heavy with the smell of something they call Purple; it didn't matter what they called it. Merci didn't like the way it made her friends act; it was like they lost all their ladylike qualities, and all they did was giggle and eat. Whenever they smoked it, she wanted nothing to do with it. "Can't you guys go one day without smoking that stuff?" she asked, and all at once, said in perfect unison, "No."

 "Come on, Fatima, I gotta go to the cleaner. Walk with me," Merci said. "No, I'll wait here for you," she gave her that I'm going to smoke look, so Merci started to walk away when one of the boys standing in the crowd said, "I'll walk with you." She turned around to see who it was, and she was surprised to see Adonis, a boy from her English class, standing there with a friendly smile on his face. Merci had never really talked to him before, but he seemed nice enough, so they walked in silence for a few blocks until Adonis said, "So, what are your plans for the summer?" She told him that she and her friends were just trying to find things to do and stay out of trouble. Adonis chuckled and then said, "Well, I can help you with that fun part. Have you ever been to Coney Island?"

Merci's eyes lit up; she had always heard about Coney Island but had never been there. "Nope! I haven't; what's it like?" Adonis answered, "It's like nothing you've ever seen before; trust me, you're going to love it," and with that, they made plans to go to Coney Island the following weekend. Merci couldn't wait to see what Adventures summer would bring with her new friend.

They made small talk about the neighborhood and school. Merci found herself surprised about how easy it was to talk to Adonis. Despite his rough exterior, he seemed genuinely interested in what she had to say, and he made her laugh with his quick wit.

When they arrived at the cleaners, Adonis insisted on paying for the curtains and treating Merci to that ice cream. They sat on a nearby bench, enjoying the treats. He asked Merci if she wanted to hang out later that evening. She hesitated because she knew he had a bit of a reputation around the neighborhood and didn't want to get mixed up in anything sketchy, but there was something about him that she couldn't resist; maybe it was his confidence or his rugged good looks, or the way he made her feel like the only girl in the world, finally, she said okay and that was the beginning of a summer that Merci would never forget.

The summer flew by so fast; it was already Labor Day, a week away from the first day of her second year of high school. Merci was really looking forward to it. All throughout the summer, Merci and Adonis stole whatever little time they could spend together because with her mother watching her like a hawk and his summer job in the cleaners, they saw each other once or twice a week; even with that, they had grown close, and she knew she would see more of him in school.

It was the last week of summer break, and Estelle decided to take Merci and her friends to Disneyland for 3 days. The girls were all so excited, and they went off to Disneyland with Merci and her mother. They acted like little girls, although they were 13 and 14 years old. This was an unforgettable experience. It was the first time Sariah or any of the girls had been out of the neighborhood. It was the best 3 days they had ever had. The fact that it was time to go home made them sad; they wished they could stay forever. The raindrops trickled down slowly on the window of the huge 747 jet as it taxied towards the gate. After landing, it began to pour down rain, making for a gloomy homecoming. They stood there quietly, waiting for the luggage to come down the carousel. No one said anything, but everyone felt the same: back to reality, back to the lives they so desperately wanted to forget. Merci still had Adonis to look forward to, and she found herself really missing him.

As the taxi made its way through New York City traffic on a rainy day, they exchanged stories about their favorite rides and attractions at Disneyland. Despite feeling a bit down about returning to their neighborhood, they were still excited for the start of the new school year. Merci couldn't wait to see Adonis again and was already planning what to wear on the first day of school. She knew she had to make a good impression and hoped that he felt the same way about her as she did about him.

Once they got home, making their way through the familiar streets of the neighborhood, Merci couldn't help but feel like something had changed in her over the summer. She felt more confident, surer of herself, and more determined to make something of her life. They hugged one another. "Thank you, Dr. Lowe," they said, we really had fun."

Estelle delivered them all home safely. Merci couldn't help but think that this was just the beginning of something great; she had Adonis by her side and was ready to take on whatever challenges came their way. The summer may have been over, but Merci knew that the memories she had made with her friends and the experiences she'd had would stay with her forever.

The first day of school was exciting, to say the least, but the highlight of her day was seeing Adonis during lunch. He looked good in the gray and burgundy uniform he was wearing; he really was a God in her eyes. They had lunch together, looking over their class schedules, hoping they had at least one class together.

Merci had sociology, history, and chemistry along with her remedial math and English, and Adonis had math English as well as social studies, chemistry, and Spanish. They did math together every Wednesday. So, every evening, they would study together. Estelle did not really like him; she called him a neighborhood thug; even so, Merci ignored her mother's comments about Adonis and continued to spend time with him. After school, they would do homework together and sometimes just talk about their day.

As time passed, they grew even closer, and Merci thought that she could tell him anything. Walking home from school one afternoon, Adonis stopped and took Merci's hand. "Merci, there's something I've been wanting to tell you," he said, looking nervous, feeling her heart racing as she waited for him to speak. "What is it?" she asked, trying to hide her excitement. Taking a deep breath, he said, "I really like you, Merci; I mean, I like you more than just a friend."

Merci's Heart skipped a beat; she had been hoping he would say something like this, but she was still surprised to hear it. "I like you, too, Adonis," she said, smiling as they continued walking hand in hand, feeling like they were on top of the world, and from that day on, they were officially a couple. She felt like the luckiest girl in Harlem. She couldn't believe that the boy she had been crushing on for so long actually liked her back, but their happiness was short-lived a few weeks later.

Adonis got into a fight with another boy from the neighborhood and was suspended from school for a week. Merci was devastated, missing him terribly, and constantly worried about him. When he finally returned to school, he seemed different somehow. He was more distant and moodier, and he didn't seem as interested in spending time with her. She tried to talk to him about it, but he just shrugged her off and said he was fine. Knowing something was wrong, seeing it in his eyes, Merci was determined to find out what it was. She wanted to help him in any way she could.

Her final year in high school was uneventful. Previously, they were together every day; he always walked with her from school, and anytime you saw one of them, the other wasn't far away. They were an item, but she began to feel him slipping away, and she wasn't quite sure what the reason was; she wasn't sure whether it was that he was seeing someone else or those friends of his she didn't like, especially the ones that were always attempting to steer him in the wrong direction.

Was it just that he and she were growing apart? She wasn't sure, but she was about to go on another excavation with Estelle, and she didn't know if the relationship could withstand another separation.

Embarking on another excavation trip with her mother, feeling a sense of unease about her relationship with Adonis; although she tried to push those thoughts back to the back of her mind and focus on her task, it was hard to ignore the growing distance between them. As usual, the trip was a success, and Merci returned home feeling proud of the work she accomplished, but when she saw Adonis, something felt different; he seemed distant, and when she tried to talk to him about it again, he just brushed her off.

Merci's solution was to focus on her studies. She felt more and more alone; he was spending less and less time with her, and she couldn't shake the feeling that he was seeing someone else. Merci's grades began to slip, and she found it hard to focus on anything other than her relationship. Estelle was not having it; she told Merci to end the relationship, or she would, so she finally confronted Adonis and asked him what was going on. He admitted that he had been seeing someone else but never told her who.

She felt her heartbreak, having been so vested in their relationship, and now it seemed like it was all for nothing. In the end, she realizes that she doesn't need Adonis to be happy. She had her own goals and dreams and was determined to achieve them with or without him. She knew that she was destined for greatness, so she picked herself up and focused on her own journey, ready to tackle whatever future lay ahead. Estelle took Merci with her to Cairo for an archeology conference on the latest ancient discoveries to put some distance between her and Adonis.

Returning home, Merci was excited to see Adonis again, but she was also nervous; she wasn't sure what to expect. She knew things had changed, but when she saw him, she felt a rush of emotions: joy, relief, and sadness all mixed together. She always knew that him cheating on her was a possibility, but hearing it from him made it real. Trying to be strong, she couldn't help the tears that fell from her eyes.

He tried to comfort her, but she pulled away. She still needed time to process everything. Finally, she was coming to terms with the end of their relationship. Throwing herself into her schoolwork, hoping it would distract her from the pain, slowly but surely, she began to heal. She realized that she was stronger than she thought and that she didn't need anyone to define her.

This was her senior year in high school. Feeling a renewed sense of purpose, she was determined to make the most of this last year and to focus on her own goals. She didn't know what the future held, but she was ready to face it head-on. Throughout the years, while Merci was away at college, Fatima kept her updated on what was going on in the neighborhood and how Adonis was doing. Every weekend, she and Adonis would talk for hours. He apologized for what he had done and asked for her forgiveness. She forgave him, but she never trusted him again.

After Estelle's death, she returned to the home she grew up in, yearning for him, wondering where he was and what he was doing because she was now alone. The day she returned from college, she opened the door to see him standing there, and they started all over again, trying to fix what was broken. What he had broken first, he had to regain her trust, something that would be very difficult for him to do. Merci was willing to give him a chance, so before she returned to college to complete her master's, she had left him with the keys to her home and access to her inheritance; this was her way of letting him know she was trying to trust him again.

It was 7:00 a.m. when she woke up; again, she attempted to reach Adonis, but there was still no answer. Where is he? Merci wondered, continuing to get ready for class. She couldn't be late; that was one of her pet peeves. She valued her time and other people's. Making it a point to always be early to class, looking at the time on her phone, she was early, so she tried Adonis again. As she approached the building, she saw the cancellation letter on the door, so instead of returning home, she decided to go to the library and do some research. She wanted to research the Anunnaki and the ancient Sumerians more because this prophecy had consumed her mother's life. Just out of curiosity, she wanted to know why.

Hurrying across campus to her pottery analysis class, she again tried calling Adonis, but again, there was no answer; she had not spoken to him since she left New York. Now, she was very worried, trying one more time; this time, she called the house, and on the third ring, she got an answer.

"Hello," said the female voice on the other end.

"Who's this?' asked Merci.

"Who's this?" asked the voice on the other end of the phone. Merci recognized the voice; it was Fatima.

Merci responded, "This is the person whose phone you're answering."

"Oh, hi Merci, this is Fatima."

"I'm aware of that," she said, "but why are you answering my phone? And where is Adonis?"

"He's downstairs with the installers.'

"What installers?" asked Merci.

"The ones installing the equipment," was Fatima's answer.

Merci's frustration grew at the multiple attempts to find out who the installers were, what equipment they were installing, and why movers were involved, too, but Fatima said, "I'll tell Adonis to call you," and then the call ended abruptly, and it left Merci with even more questions than before. What was going on in her house, and why was Adonis so unreachable? Most of all, she wanted to know why Fatima was answering her phone. Her anger was building, and Merci couldn't shake the feeling that something was wrong.

When she got to class, she was 20 minutes late; her professor looked at her as if to say don't make it a habit. Before she could take a seat, her phone began to ring. She excused herself, with her professor looking on in disgust caused by her constant interruptions.

"What's going on?" Merci asked as soon as she heard his voice, "Why are you moving, and what are you installing?"

"Hey baby, I cleaned out the rest of your mom's room, and I'm putting them in storage."

"In a storage, why?"

"Because I'm putting the equipment for the studio in there."

"So, you brought equipment? How much did you spend?"

"About $25,000."

"Why would you spend that much? You know that that's for my tuition," she was now, passed pissed.

"Baby, don't worry, I'll put it back in time for you to pay it."

"How? Adonis, how are you putting it back?"

Hearing the anger in her voice, he tried to speak, but she continued, "So there's only $5,000 left?" she asked.

"Yea," he answered.

"We will discuss this later," she said as she hung up the phone.

A little voice in her head said, "You are no one's fool."

Dialing Estelle's lawyer immediately, Merci told him to find a way to release the $150,000 she was to receive after graduation since it was only 5 months away. Telling him she hoped that he would release it.

"Ms. Lowe, I'd like to make you aware that I am receiving payment from your mother's estate to continue as your attorney if you would like?"

She thought about it for a second, then agreed to the arrangement, and he agreed to release the $150,000. He was now her attorney, so she instructed him to put this money into a separate account only she could access.

"Okay, Miss Lowe, I'll take care of it right away," he said, "by the way, Miss Lowe, you also have rental property income."

"Excuse me, what's that?" she asked.

"It means you own the building you live in and have paying tenants."

"Wow!" she said, "what exactly is in that account?"

Pausing before answering her, he said, "If I recollect correctly, it's about $750,000, maybe a million."

"A million dollars are you serious?" she said.

He laughed and replied, "Yes."

"Well, are there any other accounts that I'm not aware of?"

There was a little sarcasm present. "Yes," he replied, "there are several; when you come into the city, stop by my office. I'll explain everything to you, okay?"

Before she said goodbye, Merci said, "Sir, please don't forget the first account I put my boyfriend's name on; make sure that the bank does not release any more funds from that account without my consent. Thank you," and hung up.

Almost forgetting where she was and trying to maintain her composure, she jumped 10 feet off the ground, screaming I'm rich, I'm rich, and several people passing by looked at her as if she was crazy; she really didn't care. Thinking out loud, her mind racing, *I don't have any classes tomorrow, so I'll drive to New York and do a little shopping.*

After ending the call, she just couldn't shake the feeling in her stomach. She trusted Adonis with her mother's belongings, and now, he had taken a large chunk of her money and spent it on equipment for his studio. It would have been different if he had talked to her about it, but to just take it without her consent left a bitter taste in her mouth.

Leaving the classroom, she decided to take the rest of the day off and go to New York. She wanted to see exactly what was going on. Merci loved Adonis very much for a very long time, believing that love was an unconditional commitment to an imperfect being. Loving Adonis was not just a feeling; it was her conscious judgment; an eternal promise she wanted to keep.

Deciding to make a night of it, she went to Victoria's Secrets and got something really sexy. She wanted to surprise him and show him that she was trying to make the adjustment after losing her mom. Stopping by Bath and Body Works and getting some candles, she loved the way they smelled. What a romantic night without some bubbly, so she grabbed a bottle of champagne. *"I think I want some Moet Rose. Tonight, it was on and popping,"* she said, laughing to herself. By the time she finished shopping, it was late; she started uptown to Harlem, driving through these streets reminded her of the joy this place held for her but also reminded her of the pain. Still, Harlem was home.

The kids were running around, playing in the water hydrant at 11 pm, spraying her car with water as she drove past; *only in New York*, she said, laughing inside. Music blaring loudly, playing Marvin Gaye's What's Going On; the summer was in full effect. Her mind continued to wander back to Adonis, wondering what he had spent $25,000 on.

Pulling up in front of the building, instead of feeling like a homecoming, there was a feeling of dread; again, there it was, that feeling she was becoming familiar with, her stomach and the added nervousness. Still, she kept ignoring it, trying not to pay it any mind, but soon, she would realize it was her warning system.

She removed her bags, distinctively looked up towards Fatima's window and started upstairs. From the third floor, she could hear music playing, but otherwise, it was unusually quiet, and *where was her Bestie? She was always hanging out the window. Maybe she found something to do with her life,* laughing at the thought. Stopping to catch her breath, Merci wondered, *"But wait, why is he playing Fire and Desire? That's our song, "Oh, he must really miss me,* so rather than ring the bell, she used her key. Smelling food cooking and laughing to herself, *Adonis cooking?* Trying to be quiet, she snuck into the kitchen and was immediately angered at what she saw. "Fatima, what the hell are you doing in my kitchen?"

"Oh s***, you scared me, Merci," she said.

"You haven't answered my question, and where is Adonis?" Fatima motioned towards the bedroom as Merci walked away, and she said, "Find something more appropriate to wear around my man, and what the hell are you doing here? Go home."

Walking into the bedroom, she found Adonis stretched out on the bed in his boxers. "Baby, what is taking so long with the food?" he said as he looked over his shoulder, and he was obviously shocked to see Merci standing there.

"Who are you calling baby, and what's going on here?" she asked, trying not to look surprised. He said, "There's nothing going on here. I asked Tima to fix me something to eat. I'm tired of eating fast food, anyway. You're never here to cook for me, and I didn't think you'd mind."

"That's your problem; you don't think," was her response. Looking him in his eyes, she left the room. She didn't trust Fatima, nor did she trust him. She didn't want to believe what her inner self was telling her. Gathering her bags, she told him he needed to go back to his parent's house, and he needed to be gone before she returned. Storming out of the room, her heart raced with the mix of anger, betrayal, and confusion.

Finally, she knew who it was that Adonis had been seeing; it was her best friend, Fatima. The realization of the situation began to settle in, and she couldn't shake off the instinct that he was so lame in his attempt to dismiss her concerns, which only fueled her suspicion further. She hardly gathered her belongings, her hands trembling with a mix of anger and hurt.

The night she had planned, filled with love and excitement, had been shattered by the sight of Fatima in her kitchen half naked and Adonis' blatant disrespect for their relationship. The trust that had once bound them was now fragile and hanging by a thread. Making her way towards the door, she turned back one last time, her eyes piercing Adonis' soul. The silence between them was deafening, laden with unspoken words and forgotten promises.

 At that moment, Merci made a choice, a choice to protect herself, reclaim her worth, and break free from the chains of love that had lost its meaning. With a determined stride, she left the apartment. The weight of her decision was bearing down on her; the world outside seemed cold and unforgiving, but deep within her, a fire was ignited. With a resemblance of strength and resilience, Merci knew that this was a turning point, the moment she would rise above the ashes and forge her own path.

When Merci stepped onto the bustling streets of New York, tears mingling with determination streamed down her cheeks. She got in her car and left behind a chapter of her life that had come to a painful end. The road ahead was uncertain, but in her heart, she knew that it was time to rediscover herself, heal, and someday embrace the love she truly deserved.

As her car carried her away, the tires rolled over the pavement, echoing the rhythm of her beating heart. Leaning back against the seat, envisioning the future, her strength and resilience would lead her to new horizons. Her journey had just begun, and she was ready. As her home faded into the distance, she took a deep breath, releasing the pain of the past and embracing the unknown, determined to rise above the ashes and emerge stronger than ever.

This night had been filled with uncertainty, but within her spirit, a flicker of her mother's light burned bright as a beacon guiding her toward the future, assured that her heart would heal and love would find its way to her again. She got back to campus and went home. Mary Ellen wasn't home, so she had the house to herself. Now, she needed some time alone with her thoughts, and all the questions she had in her head gave her a headache. "Mama," she cried, "You were my rock. Now, I feel so alone!" Merci cried until she fell asleep. Unaware that this was a small problem compared to what she would soon face.

Merci found solace in the memories of happier times with her mother, but now, loneliness was a constant companion. Deciding she would just focus on her studies and nothing else, the ringing of the phone shook her from her sleep. Who could this be at this hour? Glancing at the clock on her nightstand, she answered the phone, and it was Professor Dawson, head of the archeology Department, who quickly apologized for waking her, "Good morning, Miss Lowe, I've been trying to reach you."

"Yes, Professor, how can I help you?" she asked, wiping the cold from her eyes.

Professor Dawson continued, "One of my students has had a family emergency and had to return home. I need a replacement for him on a dig, and you were suggested; besides, I know that you have some familiarity with the site at TA-set-Neferu."

Merci, again, not fully awakened, yet the mention of the site caught her attention. It was a place she had visited with her mother, Estelle, during her childhood. Memories began flooding back, reminding her of the precious moment she had shared there with her mom, who had been her Light.

"Yes, sir, I'm familiar with the site," she replied, her voice tingling with both curiosity and caution, "but it's been years since I've been there. How can I be of help?"

The professor hesitated for a moment before continuing, "Well, I understand that you were young when you visited, but your familiarity with the site could still be valuable, and we need someone to fill in on short notice. I believe you have the potential to contribute to our research."

Merci's mind raced with conflicting thoughts; the idea of returning to the site stirred a mix of emotions within her: nostalgia, excitement, and fear. Still, it was an opportunity to reconnect with her mother's passion, along with her legacy. It also meant delving into a world that held both beauty and unknown dangers.

After a moment of contemplation, Merci made her decision, "Alright, Professor, I'll accept the opportunity to join the dig; I'll do my best to contribute in any way I can."

Hanging up the phone, her mind now fully awake and buzzing was anticipation, with the unexpected turn of events offering a chance for her to immerse herself in her mother's world and perhaps discover a deeper connection to her own identity. Still lying in bed, her mind full of thoughts of ancient artifacts, hidden tombs, and all the

Mysteries waiting to be unearthed filled her imagination.

As fate would have it, this journey would not only bring her closer to her mother's legacy but also lead her on a path intertwined with ancient secrets, unforeseen challenges, and the unraveling of her own destiny.

Chapter 8: Ishtar, Antu, Ninhursag (A Descent into Darkness)

The air grew heavy within the King's chamber as the Sebittu faded away, their presence departing as swiftly as it had arrived; their true nature revealed they were not a benevolent Council of Scholars but rather demons, creations of ancient times designed for destruction. Anu had bestowed these powerful entities upon his minister of defense, Erra, as weapons to unleash havoc upon the mortal realm.

As the realization of their true identity settled upon the room, a sinister silence enveloped the chamber. The king's gaze turned dark, betraying a hidden agenda lurking beneath this facade. The revelation of the royal child's existence, intertwined with divine lineage and cosmic implications, seemed to have awakened the dormant darkness within the king's heart. Meanwhile, Ninhursag stood before Anu, her features illuminated by another worldly glow emanating from the gold-encrusted vial she held. Within its confines lay the essence of the royal heirs' DNA pulsating with untold power.

Anu extended his hand, ready to pass the vial to Asag, a trusted servant who was about to embark on a perilous journey into the future. As the vial contacted Asag's hand, an unexpected phenomenon unfolded: it began to radiate intense light, and its golden surface glowed with brilliance. The king looked on with astonishment as he explained that luminosity would guide their path, leading them closer to the elusive royal heir.

The child's very essence escapes from this vial, attaching itself to her and revealing her identity. However, amidst the unfolding events, the king became increasingly unhinged, and his motives became increasingly apparent, especially since he summoned the Sebittu. The true nature of the Sebittu, their demonic origins, and their purpose as instruments of chaos threatened to plunge the mortal realm into a descent of darkness.

The king's motivation, shrouded in secret, hinted at a grander plan beyond the mere search for the royal heir. A hidden agenda lay behind his actions. As the gravity of the situation settled upon Asag and Ninhursag, a sense of apprehension filled their spirits because they understood the weight of this mission, as well as the potential ramifications of altering the delicate fabric of time, the future beckoned promising answers, but also harboring unprecedented consequences.

With determination, Asag awaited further instructions. He was prepared to venture into the darkness, guided by the radiant glow of the royal heir's DNA. Asag's journey would unravel truths beyond anyone's wildest imagination, unveiling the intricate web connecting gods and mortals, destiny and choice, the fate of the royal child, the kingdom, and the very existence of the cosmic realm held in the balance, as the Sebittu continued their search for the heir.

As he clutched the glowing vial tightly, Asag prepared for the journey. The Sebittu, the embodiment of Anu's destructive force, reveled in the annihilation of humans. Alongside them, the Hallaku belonging to the seventh House of the Fallen emerged as agents of destruction when Creations from other realms spiraled out of control or exceeded their allotted time.

In the vast expanse of the universe, there was no escaping their wrath; the heir's existence, beyond the confines of time, was now their exclusive target. As Ninhursag departed from the King's chamber, her path crossed with Antu's servant girl, Badea. "Tell your queen to come to my chambers," she said, "I have news of the king's search for the heir." The servant girl made haste to deliver the message to the queen.

Antu swiftly arrived at Ninhursag's chamber. Her Regal composure betrayed a sense of unease. "Sister," she implied, "what news do you have?" Ninhursag proceeded to reveal the King's use of the royal heir's DNA to track her down. Antu's regal facade crumbled, and her sister knew that Antu had knowledge far beyond what she had been willing to admit.

With a mixture of apprehension and determination, she confronted her sister, demanding answers. "What have you done, sister?" she questioned. Antu was aware that her sister had already faced Anu's scrutiny. She now grappled with the risk involved in telling her sister her secret, knowing that exposing Ninhursag's life to danger was a grave consequence; however, realizing that Anu's previous questioning indicated he possessed some knowledge and silence could only exacerbate the situation, Antu telepathically told her sister that they should communicate as they did as children, ensuring their conversation remained shielded from prying ears.

Bound by the responsibilities of the kingdom and the depth of their sisterly bond, Antu took a deep breath and began to unravel a hidden truth within ancient walls, steeped in wisdom and secrecy. Antu disclosed a divine lineage of a child born who would soon come to power, their souls resonating within the sanctity of their private exchange. The mysteries of the royal heir, the cosmic realm, and their own destiny unfolded.

Together, they confronted the weight of the choice that led them to this pivotal moment—the boundaries between loyalty and betrayal, duty, and personal desires blurred as the fate of their bloodline and the heart of their reality was on the verge of unraveling. In the depth of their shared understanding, Antu and Ninhursag forged an unspoken pack to safeguard the secret, protect the kingdom, and, ultimately, guide the royal heir through the enigmatic path of her destiny.

With the weight of this hidden knowledge and the weight of their realm's survival, they vowed to navigate the treacherous waters of uncertainty; their bond and the secret they would now share threatened to reshape the course of history itself.

As the echoes of their shared understanding reverberated within, they steadied themselves for the heavy burden and challenges that lay ahead. Their intertwined fate was now entangled with the enigma of the royal heir, and this propelled them forward into a future laden with both danger and redemption. These ancient walls would remain silent witnesses, guarding their whispered truths and awaiting the moment when their world would be shaken to its core.

Ninhursag understood her sister's request. These two shared a deep understanding, born from their upbringing in a telepathic society and in a world where secrets were impossible to keep. The sister goddesses devised a private language, communicating solely with each other through coded telepathy that allowed them to speak freely, shielding their conversation from prying ears as the queen unraveled her hard-wrenching revelations; her sister's empathy sensed her anguish.

Antu began to tell her sister of the child she was willing to die to save. Antu could not only see, but she felt her sister's fear because now Ninhursag knew what would happen if Anu found Merci before her 21st birthday. Together, they had to think of ways to warn Merci of the imminent danger, and it was approaching fast; they had to get a message to her without creating suspicion. Antu considered returning to the Future, just long enough to prepare her daughter and give her a chance to survive, but decided to send for their younger sister, Ishtar, who was on Earth at her Temple, which the humans had just completed, and they were dedicating it to her.

The time was 5000 BC, and the Sumerians were technologically advanced people who had been taught math and science by the gods. These two are the language of the universe, they are the key to the survival of mankind. As they awaited Ishtar's arrival, Antu understood the path ahead was treacherous and full of uncertainties: the fate of their bloodline and the future of humanity was at stake. United by a shared determination, they vowed to safeguard Merci and to deliver her from the pending storm while navigating the intricate dance between divine intervention and modern free will.

In the depths of their sisterly bond and their connection to the nature of mankind, Antu and Ninhursag knew that Anu prepared to unleash a series of events that would reverberate through time itself. A message had to be sent: a warning encrypted within the fabric of human progress ensuring Merci's survival.

They had to do this without arousing suspicion, solidified in their hearts, heavy with the weight of their secret.

They braced themselves for the trial that awaited them and the pivotal role they were playing in shaping the destiny of the royal heir as well as the course of human history. Ishtar heard her sister's call and hurried to their side. "Why have you sent for me?" she asked her sisters as they began to explain to her that Anu had sent the Hallaku and the Sebittu in search of Merci using her DNA and that she didn't have much time.

Immediately, Ishtar said, "Use the portal at Ur." "No," said Antu because the king would be watching for any shift in the time space continuum, and that would lead him straight to Merci; they could not take that chance. Her dreams finished. "Ishtar, I taught her our secret language. "We can send her a message in her dreams," so they put their plans into action.

The Hallaku started their search in the current time and tracked the royal heir's scent to the temple of Enlil in Ur but lost it; that had never happened before. *Had she been here in this time?* Asag thought to himself. He hated the stench of the humans; all they were good for, in his eyes, was their life force. Asag often wondered why Anu hadn't destroyed them all but was allowing them to grow in numbers and advance into a technologically advanced civilization. It was a puzzle to him; there was no purpose for the existence of humans except as a vessel for their life force, a resource that sustained immortals.

Ishtar went deep into the supernatural realm, harnessing her divine power to connect with Merci through her dreams; in the depths of her sleep, Merci would receive the message encoded within the sacred language known only to the goddesses. Ishtar was resolute, embracing her role of guiding Merci towards destiny.

The Hallaku continued their relentless search, following the faint Trail of the royal heir's essence. The journey led them to an Ancient Temple at Ur, where their tracking faulted, and the scent dissipated. Perplexed and confused, Asag again questioned if the heir had indeed been present at this time. Still, human existence disgusted him.

As the pieces of the grand tapestry were set in motion, the threads of fate began to intertwine Anu's relentless pursuit, the goddesses' clandestine effort to protect Merci, and the cosmic forces at play all danced in a delicate balance.

The clock ticked relentlessly with each passing moment, bringing Merci closer to her destiny. Unbeknownst to her, her life would be irrevocably altered by forces beyond her comprehension. The ancient divinity intertwined with the mortal realm, along with the veil of time and space, were now blurred. As the wheels of fate turned, the key to unlocking her true purpose was within Merci, soon to receive a revelation that would set her on a path of unimaginable significance.

In the shadows, Anu observed unfolding events. The cosmos trembled, and all celestial beings held their breath, for the fate of one mortal tied to the divinity within her held the power to shape the fabric of existence. The realm held its breath, bracing for the revelation and trials that lay ahead.

The royal heir's scent was very different; it had a sweet aroma to it. Asag had never come across anything like it. It had a value much more than any life force he had encountered before. He was sure that he could find it anywhere in the universe, in any dominion, at any time from creation to eternity; he was going to find her.

Many questions remained in Anu's head. *Is this child my enemy? Has she evolved as was suggested? Is she just another step in the evolution of humanity? Or was she born of a royal female in my house? Have I been so blind that I did not see? "If so, they will all have hell to pay," he said,*

"I will watch the Hallaku and the Sebittu destroy them one by one, piece by piece."

The plan was coming together, and time was not on their side. Someone would have to distract the king long enough for them to astral project themselves to Merci to instruct, prepare, and strengthen her for the Battle of her life. *Poor child* thought Ishtar. Merci had no idea what was headed her way, and there was no way to stop it.

She just needed to be ready, and if anyone could get her ready, the Goddess of War would be the one to do it. The weight of the mission hung heavy on the goddesses' shoulders; they strategized their next move. They knew they had to act swiftly, for time was a merciless adversary.

Antu, Ninhursag, and Ishtar convened in a secluded chamber, their minds brimming with determination and a shared sense of responsibility. Antu, attempting to remain regal and graceful in her wisdom, pondered the most effective approach to divert her husband's attention; she knew she had to exploit the complexities of divine politics to buy Ishtar time. Requiring a delicate dance of manipulation and persuasion, a gamble that could tip the scales in their favor.

Ninhursag suggested utilizing the mortal realms and making connections to the natural world. She proposed orchestrating a grand ceremony, a celebration of life, and the bounties of nature to captivate the king's focus. It would be a spectacle of such magnificence that even the great king would find it difficult to resist. Ishtar, her essence pulsating with the essence of war and strategy, contemplated the impending confrontation Merci would soon face.

She analyzed her ancient knowledge, drawing upon her vast experience in battles far across the universe, with a plan to awaken Merci's dormant powers while training her in the ways of combat and defend against the encroaching evil.

The sisters knew that their tasks would not be easy. Anu's power and influence reached far and wide, and his obsession with locating the royal heir threatened their carefully laid plan, but their love for Merci and the commitment to safeguard her future ignited an unyielding determination within them. This cosmic thread of destiny entwines the lives of mortals and immortals alike.

Merci, still unaware of her true nature and the perils that awaited her, stood at the Pinnacle of a monumental Journey. The goddesses summoned their strength, channeling the divine energy that flowed within them, and with unwavering resolve, embarked on this mission that would test their bond, challenge their abilities, and shape the destiny of worlds.

The celestial dance had begun, and Merci, the unsuspecting protagonist, would soon be thrust into a world where gods and mortals collided in a confrontation for the very essence of existence. Amidst the cosmic upheaval and the clashing of powers, the fate of Merci and the universe had begun a precocious dance. The goddesses, bound by their secret language and unyielding love, would strive to guard and protect Merci from the shadows hidden while preparing her for the inevitable trials that awaited her. The wheels of destiny turned, and the stage for a grand confrontation was set; this would dictate their legacy in history.

"Danger, Merci," is what she heard before she opened her eyes to a vision of a beautiful ethereal Estelle standing before her, a presence that radiated power and wisdom. Estelle/ Ishtar resembled a true warrior goddess from the heights of Mount Olympus. Merci's heart swelled with a mixture of awe and longing as she called out "Mama," but Estelle stopped her, her voice both gentle and resolute, filled the room, "My child, you cannot touch me; I've already ascended this Earthly realm and have returned to my celestial home, among the stars. I am only the guardian entrusted with your care and protection until the arrival of the one who stands before us now."

Merci's gaze shifted; her eyes widened in recognition and astonishment as Antu stepped forward, embodying the radiant beauty of an angel. "N2," Merci whispered, remembering the name from her dreams. The air seemed to thicken with anticipation as the weight of their presence settled down upon the room. Merci felt a mix of reverence and fear, realizing now that her existence held a profound purpose, one that transcended her own understanding.

Antu regal and commanding addresses Merci directly, "My darling daughter, I know you must have countless questions, and they will be answered in due time; however, the urgency of the present situation demands your immediate attention. You are in grave danger. I want you to know that I have always loved you deeply and have always watched over you. Merci, you are the gift I have bestowed upon humanity, yet there are those who seek your destruction, threatening calamity like none witnessed since the dawn of creation."

Merci's mind was frantically filled with disbelief. Along with the weight of an extraordinary burden. "But how? How am I supposed to save mankind? I'm only…" Ishtar's voice interrupted her, her words hanging in the air. "It is within you, Merci; deep within your being is the strength and the power needed to defend yourself and to ensure the survival of humanity. Trust no one, please, for the peril that approaches will test your strength and power. We can only guide and prepare you, but the ultimate responsibility rests within you."

A heaviness enveloped the room as the weight of her destiny settled upon her shoulders. The fate of mankind now lay in her hands, an unimaginable task for someone who had always seen herself as ordinary, yet she always knew deep down that she possessed an extraordinary potential, a hidden strength waiting to be unleashed. As the goddesses stood before her, their celestial presence presented her with a sense of purpose and determination. She had to face the impending danger, having to go deep into the very depths of her being and embrace the role now thrust upon her.

Oblivious to the fact that the path she was about to take would test her in ways she could never imagine.

Her future held a journey of self-discovery, sacrifice, and the unyielding fight for the survival of mankind in the face of unimaginable darkness and danger.

Chapter 9: Chaos "La 'fete"

The relentless search for the royal heir led Erra and Asag across countless realms within the vast expanse of the universe. These demons were feared and reviled. They scouted through time and space, leaving behind a trail of terror while possessing unsuspecting humans and feeding on their essence, all in pursuit of their elusive target.

Strange and gruesome deaths remained unsolved, often attributed to the occult. Still, the majority went undocumented. Erra was growing increasingly frustrated as he stared at the bottle of DNA he held in his hands; it seemed useless, having failed to lead them to the royal one that they sought.

 As they approached the 20th century, a faint glow emanated from the vial as prophesied by the king. Finally, they had a breakthrough. As they neared the royal one's timeline, Asag became enraptured by the scent surrounding her.

Upon receiving the update, Anu's initial Instinct was to order her destruction; however, after a conversation with his eldest son, Enlil, a different perspective emerged, and

Enlil's wisdom urged caution and consideration, there is the possibility that she might not be an enemy, what if she was as suggested a product of mankind's evolution.

Despite the uncertainties, she remained of royal blood, and until her true nature was known, destruction was not an option. Enlil foresaw a potential advantage in the situation; what if they could bring her to their side? After all, they were still engaged in a war against Allanu's factions. She might prove to be the key to securing victory, but the prospect of harnessing her power rather than eliminating it presented a tantalizing possibility for them both.

As Asag and Erra pressed on, driven by their own agenda, a complex web of tensions and alliances began to form. The fate of the royal heir balanced at a tipping point with multiple forces vying for control and awaiting the moment of revelation that would shape the destiny of not only the heir but the entire cosmos.

Enlil could see his words made sense to his father, yet his motives were not out of concern for the royal heir; but of how he could possibly use her to steal his father's kingdom. After all, the prophecy stated she would rule through eternity, making controlling her a benefit; therefore, he wanted to see if he could bring her over to his side; if not, he'd destroy her himself.

Enlil is part of the Celestial Trinity; he is the god of the air. His brother, Enki, was the god of the water, and Anu was their father and ruler of the Galaxy. Just being the god of the air wasn't enough; for Enlil, he wanted to rule the whole kingdom, and the royal heir would help him achieve that goal; her life depended on it. Anu's love of mankind made Enlil hate them, and his father knew that the creation of mankind would someday be their undoing.

Feeling that his father was an old man with little left to offer the kingdom, he was from a time long gone. His father's time on the throne was over; Enlil waited for the day he would take the kingdom for himself. Little did he know his brother, Enki, was watching.

Merci hurried through the airport; a surge of anxiety gripped her, hoping that she hadn't missed her flight. By a stroke of luck, she reached the gate just before they closed the boarding doors. Taking a breath, she was escorted to her seat by a friendly stewardess; however, in the flurry of the moment, an envelope slipped from her bag, falling onto the floor. She bent down to pick it up, suddenly realizing it was a letter from Dr. Azizi.

This intrigued her. As she read its contents, the world of genetics and DNA unfolded before her. These words revealed secrets and mysteries that had long been kept hidden. Each sentence unraveled a new layer of questions about her identity and purpose. Merci's heart raced as she absorbed the staggering truths revealed in the letter. She was no ordinary young woman; she held within her the power to shape existence itself.

The weight of this revelation settled upon her shoulders, mingling with the sense of both curiosity and fear. With each passing word, the letter became her guidebook to a world she had never imagined. A mix of fear and uncertainty filled Merci's heart. Gazing out through the airplane window, she contemplated the magnitude of her newfound destiny, knowing this journey would be perilous, filled with tests.

Merci knew she could not turn away, vowing to uncover the truth about herself and fulfill her ultimate purpose. The fate of the world and the universe was heavy. The letter read: "Dear Dr. Lowe, after careful examination of your daughter's blood work, I have found strange anomalies which have never been seen in humans in our history, causing me to further investigate her DNA makeup. In doing so, I found that she does not have the usual double helix but a triple helix. This, Dr. Lowe, is a great discovery. I would like to further study your daughter. Please contact me as soon as possible. Thank you, Dr. Azizi."

Looking at the date on the letter, she realized that Estelle had received this letter before she died. *"What is really going on here?"* she asked, *"was that just a dream yesterday, or was someone really trying to tell me something?"* Remembering the names of the two women she had seen in her dream, she went online and started to research who they were. She was surprised by what she found.

They were indeed deities from the ancient Sumerian times, believed to be the gods of Heaven. Suddenly, this feeling of immense fear came over her. Was she really in danger, and why? The flight from New York to Cairo seemed to stretch endlessly, with Merci feeling the weight of exhaustion and the disorienting effects of jet lag. All she yearned for was a moment of rest, a rest from the mountain of confusion and revelations that had consumed her thoughts. Upon the plane touching down, she could already sense the ancient mysteries and timeless wonders that awaited her in the land of the Pharaohs.

The school's representative greeted Merci at the airport and whisked her away to the Heliopolis Hotel in Cairo. It was here that the Expedition team would gather before embarking on their journey to Luxor the following morning. The hotel provided a brief sanctuary, a place for Merci to collect her thoughts and prepare herself for the challenges that lay ahead.

The expedition group arrived at the sacred site the following morning, and Merci felt a surge of familiarity rush over her. The Valley of the Queens, known as Ta-set-Neferu, was a place of serene beauty, a sanctuary for the wives and daughters of the Pharaohs. Within its tombs, these royal women were laid to rest. Their final resting places filled with treasures and riches befitting their esteemed lineage.

 Among the myriads of tombs and structures that dotted the landscape, there stood an enigmatic structure, an introverted pyramid that defied conventional understanding; its construction was a testament to the Ingenuity and skill of the ancient people, a marvel that left Merci amazed. Yet despite years of excavation and exploration, no entrance had ever been discovered until now.

The Expedition team had uncovered the entrance to this extraordinary structure. A moment that held the promise of unveiling untold secrets while shedding light on the enigmatic past. Merci, like her mother before her, possessed the unique gift of deciphering ancient writings and languages.

Merci examined the inscriptions that were filling the walls, noticing something unprecedented in the field of archeology: words containing a mix of hieroglyphics and cuneiform, the emergence of two ancient writing systems. The implications of this discovery were profound. Valley of the Queens held more than the riches and remains of royal women; it held a profound connection to the divine and the celestial realm.

Merci's heart raced with anticipation and a tinge of trepidation. Wondering what mysteries awaited her within the depths of this extraordinary structure and what role this would play in unraveling the secrets of her own lineage. The morning sunlight drenched the valley in soft golden Hues. Merci was now ready to embark on a journey that would test her courage as well as her faith.

The Valley of The Queens was not just a place of beauty but a crucible of destiny, where her true purpose awaited.

Each step forward, embracing the weight of her ancestry, she was determined to honor the legacy of the royal women who had come before her. To unlock the timeless truths that lay hidden within the heart of Ta-set-Neferu. Carbon dating dated this pyramid to around 8,000 BC; it had been buried and sealed at that time. The first question on Merci's mind was why? And what were the ancients attempting to lock away? As she looked at the inscription, she recognized the sign of danger that was written in hieroglyphics and cuneiform.

Taking a picture of the inscription with her cell phone, she wanted to be sure that she was interpreting it correctly. Beginning with the eight-pointed star and lion scepter, Merci was aware that this was a symbol of the goddess Ishtar, knowing immediately she needed to go to the Temple of the Goddess Ishtar.

Merci quickly relayed this to the professor, and off she went to Babylon; she knew this was no regular pyramid but an eternal prison for something, and before they opened it, they needed to know what. "Wow!" Merci couldn't get over the fact that, here again, was the goddess Ishtar.

As she made the journey to the ruins of Uruk, having the distinct feeling this had something to do with her. Reading all the mythology surrounding Ishtar, she began to understand what Ishtar/Estelle had said to her in a dream, that she was the only one who had protected her until a time such as this.

Making her way to the ruins of Eturkalamma, Merci pondered the connection between the pyramid and the goddess Ishtar. The echoes of her dream resounded in her mind, reminding her again of Ishtar's words that she had been protected until a pivotal moment in time, which was now.

This journey to the location of the Goddess Ishtar's Temple gate felt like a steppingstone towards unraveling the enigma that surrounded her. During her research, she dug deep into ancient knowledge about Ishtar, emerging her in a rich tapestry of myth and Legend. She sought to piece together the puzzle, hoping to decipher the significance of Ishtar's involvement and to understand her own role in this intricate tapestry of fate.

As she dug deeper into Ishtar's mythology, fragments of memories began to resurface, linking her to a divine purpose that lay before her. Estelle/ Ishtar rather, Estelle, in her dream, had foreseen this moment and had shielded Merci until the time was right.

With each step, Merci was determined to unearth the truth and honor her mother's legacy while fulfilling the destiny that awaited her. At the Temple of Ishtar, the answers she needed lay within these ancient walls. Merci was determined to uncover the secrets that would bring clarity to her own identity as well as the pyramid's hidden purpose.

It had been a week since Merci left for Egypt. She had finally pieced together the meaning behind the inscription. It revealed a tale of a celestial battle between the goddess Ishtar and the demon Asmodeus, who had been banished and imprisoned within the inverted pyramid. Aware that great danger lay ahead, Merci urgently tried to contact Professor Dawson, trying to warn him against opening the pyramid; however, her attempts went unanswered, leaving her concerned that the unimaginable had been unleashed upon the world.

Now, with the knowledge of their formidable foe, Merci felt a sense of urgency to uncover a way to stop Asmodeus. Fear plagued her thoughts, realizing the daunting task of confronting such a powerful demon.

Retrieving that information meant she'd have to return to the ruins of the temple of Ishtar.

While deciphering the cuneiform and hieroglyphics inscribed on the temple walls, Merci became immersed in the story of love, desire, and revenge. Ishtar, the Goddess of Love and War, had been enamored with the hero, Gilgamesh. He rejected her marriage proposal, revealing the threat posed by Asmodeus, a demon consumed by lust for her, and a determination to prevent any other from possessing her.

Infuriated by this revelation, Ishtar devised a plan to trick and subdue the demon, ultimately binding and imprisoning him in an inverted pyramid in the desert. Merci's mind shifted to understanding how Ishtar had managed to bind the demon, but as she continued deciphering the ancient writings, a sense of unease enveloped her, and the feeling of being watched intensified, causing her to look over her shoulder.

In the darkness, shadows seemed to lurk, and a sense of impending danger loomed over her. Initially gripped by fear, she found herself responding with a grim sense of humor, recognizing the cliché truth of the black girl being the first victim in the horror movie.

Yet the situation became all too real, escalating her fear suddenly. An unsettling odor permeated the temple ruins, and Merci felt a touch on her hair like a whispering breeze.

An invisible presence was toying with her, remaining elusive in her sight, gathering her resolve and trying to concentrate, focusing her eyes to detect any form. Gradually, a humanoid figure with a tail begins to materialize, only to fade away again. Confusion and panic overwhelmed her as she attempted to flee, but her escape was cut short by an excruciating pain surge in her abdomen as if a dagger had been thrust into it.

Collapsing to the ground, blood scattering everywhere, desperately clinging to the notion of survival. During the assault, Merci fought back with all her strength, even though her invisible assailant remained elusive. Amid the chaos, the word focus echoed in her mind, urging her to find a way to see her attacker and increase her chances of survival.

Merci's head was pounding, and her vision blurred; she struggled to maintain focus, wiping away the blood impairing her sight. While attempting to gain control, she balanced herself against a nearby wall adorned with ancient inscriptions. To her surprise, a surge of power coursed through her as her hand made contact temporarily emboldened her. Despite the relentless attack, Merci refused to surrender; she only needed to see her attacker to understand its movements and its weaknesses.

Through sheer determination, she managed to catch a glimpse of the shadowy figure within the darkness, realizing its intangibility. Seizing a handful of sand, she hurled it at the figure, briefly exposing its movements and granting her a fleeting opportunity to escape. The sand temporarily allowed Merci to see her attacker; she could also see that it had blinded him. Now was the time to make her move, but she couldn't because the pain in her back and her leg wouldn't let her.

She cried out, "Mother, if you can hear me, I need you; I will die if you do not help me now." Lifting herself from the ground, Merci again touched the wall, and immediately, her strength was renewed. Standing tall and now looking for her attacker, Merci was not going to let whatever this was get the best of her. She had lost sight of it, but remembering what her mother had said that she was special and that there were untapped powers within her, she knew she needed to find those powers now.

"If only I could move as fast as the wind," she thought, and then, noticing that a strong wind started to blow, feeling her life being taken from her, she blacked out. When Merci woke up, she wasn't sure where she was; all she was sure of was the fact that her body was in intense pain.

 A growing crowd had gathered outside the building, drawn to it by the unsettling news of a heinous murder on the 4th floor.

The homicide detectives maneuvered through the curious onlookers, their presence sending ripples of unease through the crowd. Entering the building, the whispers and murmurs seem to follow them, creating an eerie atmosphere. Inside the apartment, darkness enveloped the space, accompanied by a chilling aura and the stench of death. The detectives exchanged glances with the other offices, sensing that something unusual had occurred here.

On the floor lay the lifeless body of a young man, his organ set neatly beside him, puzzlingly; there were no visible entrance or exit wounds on his body. The detectives inquired about other bodies, only to be met with a silent gesture pointing towards the young woman sitting in the corner, her mind seemingly unreachable; she was in a catatonic state.

Questions swirled in the detectives' minds, contemplating what horrifying sight the woman had witnessed that led her to her current condition. For now, they had to prioritize her well-being and postpone the questioning until later. EMS arrived to transport her to the hospital while the crime scene investigation unit meticulously processed the area, securing her hands, feet, and hair to prevent any potential evidence from being contaminated. With caution, the detectives moved through the crime scene, careful not to disturb any crucial findings.

On the dresser, they discovered the victim's wallet, revealing his identity as Adonis Lee Richardson, a 23-year-old from New Jersey. The apartment, however, did not belong to him; it was registered under the name of Dr. Estelle Lowe, who had passed away. According to the neighbors, Dr. Lowe's daughter, Merci, and her boyfriend lived there, yet the young woman found in the apartment turned out to be Fatima Fisher, Merci's best friend and neighbor.

With Merci being away at college, this left the detectives eager to hear Fatima's account of what transpired within these walls. As the detectives exited the building, one of them couldn't help but notice two figures standing across the street, dressed in all black with dark shades on. They were observing the detective's every move, and this raised an unsettling feeling; chuckling to himself, amused by the presence of Men in Black but wondering how much strange this situation could become.

The hospital provided no help because Miss Fisher remained heavily sedated and inaccessible for questioning. The detectives left a request with the doctor in charge, urging him to inform them as soon as she woke up. Their curiosity shifted towards Merci, leading them to drive to Penn State University. However, upon arrival, they discovered the scene swarming with campus police and other law enforcement officials.

The familiar scent of death permeated the air, mirroring the apartment where Adonis had met his demise. Inside the premises, they encountered a terrified survivor, identified as Merci's roommate, Mary Ellen. It became apparent that Merci was currently on an excavation in the Egyptian desert.

The detectives sought permission to speak with Mary Ellen, who, despite her fear, managed to provide some answers. She recounted her horrifying experience, mentioning how she had seen someone standing behind the bath shower curtain, assuming it was her boyfriend. But when she pulled the curtain back, no one was there. Moments later, she heard her boyfriend screaming for help, running from the bathroom. She witnessed him being tossed around the living room like a ragdoll by an invisible force.

In shock, she saw him collide with the wall despite there being no apparent presence. "Here, this invisible presence is again," said the detective to his partner as Mary Ellen continued, "Terrified, I ran outside and asked the neighbor to call the police. When I returned, my boyfriend was…" she paused for a second because she couldn't bring herself to say the word, continuing to speak with tears in her eyes. She said, his insides were beside him. By now, she was hysterical. The lady police officer gently took her to EMS.

Chapter 10: Asmodeus

The detectives were perplexed by the bizarre nature of the incidents and their connection to Merci. Jokingly, one detective mentioned the unfortunate fate of Miss Lowe's roommates, as they had a tendency not to live long. With a combined investigative experience of 50 years, these two detectives were astonished by the inexplicable occurrences.

Something deeply unusual was unfolding, seemingly revolving around Merci. So, they decided to depart from traditional police procedure and consult with an expert in the occult, hoping to shed light on the enigma. The looming question remained: why was there no blood found at either crime scene? Why was there no physical evidence or trace of a perpetrator? This mystery was far beyond the realms of normalcy.

The detectives ventured through the Labyrinth called the streets of New York. Eventually, they found their way through the maze and arrived at a hidden shop tucked away in a conspicuous corner. Eluding an eerie ambiance, inviting only those who sort it out. This place houses secrets and knowledge that surpasses ordinary comprehension.

These two detectives were stepping into the realm of the occult, where they hoped to find answers to the inexplicable phenomenon that surrounded Merci. Little did they know that the path they were embarking on was leading them deeper into a web of ominous suspense, where the boundaries between reality and the supernatural would blur. If you weren't looking for this place, it wouldn't particularly be on your shopping list because it was not for your average Shopper; it was a specialty store.

Anything having to do with witchcraft, sorcery, or the occult can be found here. Walking into the store, a young woman behind the counter said, "Hello, gentleman, I've been expecting you." Both detectives looked surprised. "How can I help you?" she asked. The detective, who smelled like cigars, said, "If you've been expecting us, then you already know why we're here."

"Well, yes, I actually do know why you're here; you're here because of all the strange deaths and murders throughout the city, am I correct?"

"You tell me," said the detective.

"Well," she continued, "what I can tell you is that what has been unleashed on this world has not been seen since the beginning of time. They are of the House of the Fallen; they search for the one who has come to save mankind."

"Wait," said the detective at the beginning of time, the Fallen. The fallen what?"

"Are you a man of religion?" the lady asked the Detective, "The Fallen are Angels who were cast out of heaven," said the shopkeeper, "Hell has now come upon man with a vengeance."

"Who is supposed to be saving mankind, and from what are they saving us?"

"There's one who was created by the Gods, who will save mankind or destroy it."

"And who might that be?" asked the Detective, but she continued not answering his question, "The time has come upon us that all will be revealed; we will learn truths that we had not known. The things that have been hidden forever, the truth about the origins of man, the truth about the creation of the heavens and the earth, and about the forces of good and evil. They will all soon battle fiercely for the souls of men and full control of the Earth."

"Are you talking about aliens?" asked the detective.

"Okay, time to leave," he said.

"No, wait," said the other detective, "I still have some questions; first, why are the victim's eyes and organs being removed? And why is there no blood at the scene or in the victim's bodies, and, most of all, why has nobody seen anyone or anything?"

"As I told you," she said, "these are demons of old; they are bloodthirsty, and they feed on the essence of human life. They are in the wind and in the air. They cannot be caught; they are called the Hallaku and the Sebittu. The reason for the removal of the organs is because they only want the life force. The organs are of no use to them, and the eyes are removed so that they can see what the victim has seen. Whoever they are searching for is in grave danger, and this world is in trouble until they find them. These are the destroyers of that that were created by the Gods but got out of control or ran out of time."

"Thank you," said the detectives as they left more confused than when they arrived. "Is this real?" one of them asked the other, both shaking their heads. Because of this, there are going to be a lot more bodies. How could they tell anyone this? They'd be placed in the crazy house. For now, they kept it to themselves. The one thing they didn't know was that Merci was the key.

As the detectives left the occult shop, their minds were filled with a jumble of information, as well as unanswered questions. The shopkeeper's words lingered in their thoughts, painting a chilling picture of the ancient forces at play. They couldn't deny the strangeness of the recent deaths and the absence of any tangible evidence, but to accept the existence of demons, fallen angels, and a battle for the fate of mankind seemed unthinkable.

They retreated to their squad car, driving in silence and contemplating the implications of what they had just heard. The detective who had a penance for cigars finally broke his silence, voicing his skepticism. "Are we really expected to believe all this? Demons, fallen angels, battles for souls; it sounds like something out of a horror movie," he uttered out loud, while his partner remained pensive for a moment before responding, "I don't know what to believe anymore, but one thing is clear: something unnatural is happening, and Merci Lowe is somehow connected to it all. We need to find her."

They decided to keep their encounter at the occult shop to themselves for now. Sharing such extraordinary claims could only lead to disbelief and potentially dire consequences for their careers. Instead, they focused on the tasks at hand, knowing that the clock was ticking and more lives were at stake. Back at their desk, they dug deeper into the files, attempting to connect the dots between the victims while searching for any common threads.

The removal of organs and the absence of blood remain perplexing, but now, they had a potential explanation: The insatiable hunger of the Hallaku and the Sebittu demons for the essence of human life. It sent chills down their spines, realizing that these ancient malevolent beings were on the hunt. Meanwhile, they continue to gather information on Merci, piecing together her background, her connection to the victims, and her current whereabouts. They needed to find her before the demons did.

As time went on, the investigation intensified. Every lead brought them closer to the truth but also deeper into the unknown. They couldn't shake the feeling that an invisible darkness loomed over them, watching their every move. Finally, they received the breakthrough: they needed an address to where Merci was rumored to be staying during her excavation in the Egyptian desert. The detectives wasted no time boarding a flight to Egypt, prepared to face whatever mysteries awaited them.

As they ventured into the Egyptian desert, the weight of their mission pressed upon them. The fate of mankind was teetering on a knife's edge, and they now carried the burden of protecting the key to it all, Merci. The ancient prophecies echoed in their minds, feeling the determination to confront the darkness and ensure humanity's survival. Their journey would take them deeper into the realms of the supernatural, where ancient secrets, as divine powers and unimaginable forces clash in an epic battle.

The destiny of Merci and the world hung on the brink, and they were determined to uncover the truth, no matter the costs. With the desert winds carrying whispers of ancient enigmas, the detective would be stepping into a world beyond their comprehension, and they were ready to face the unimaginable and stand against the tides of darkness that currently flowed their way.

Her body was in excruciating pain. Merci looked around, noticing a nearby fire and a selection of figs, pomegranates, and water placed beside her in a coconut shell. "Hello," she called out, seeking a response. However, as she attempted to get up, she fell back onto the animal fur she had been lying on. "Do not try to move; you have not yet healed," a voice replied. Startled, she answered, "Who's there?" unable to see anyone. The voice answered, "I am the one who saved you." Perplexed, she said quietly, "Why can't I see you?" The voice explained, "Because I am without form."

Curiosity lingering, she asked, "Where am I?"

The voice assured her, "You are in a place where those who seek to harm you cannot find you."

Needing clarity, she continued, "And who are you?"

The voice responded, "Here is not. It is void of time and space. I am Asag of the Sebittu, existing before time itself. I have brought you here to save you."

Feeling helpless and overwhelmed, she interrupted, "Why is everybody either trying to kill me or save me?"

"You are the Royal heir to the throne of the Great House of the Anunnaki!" the voice echoed with an unsettling tone, "You are not yet strong enough to defeat the approaching forces. I will guide you and reveal the truth that defines your existence. For now, you must eat because you will need all your strength."

Merci felt a chill crawl up her spine as the words hung in the air. She couldn't shake the feeling that unseen eyes were watching her every move. *Who was this enigmatic presence, and why had he brought her here?* The cryptic nature of his words and the ominous atmosphere left Merci unsettled. Doubt and fear were now her constant companion, but Merci knew she had to steady herself for the challenges ahead. She cautiously reached for the Fig and pomegranates, their sweet Aroma filling the air. As she ate, she could almost taste the ancient power that coursed through her veins.

The sustenance invigorated her, fueling a newfound determination to uncover her true purpose. The fire crackled nearby, casting dancing shadows upon the surrounding darkness. Merci spoke into the void, her voice laced with both curiosity and trepidation, "Who are you, really? Why have you brought me here? What is my role in all of this?"

An eerie silence before Asag's voice reverberated once again, "All in due time, young one, there are ancient secrets that must be unveiled and a destiny that awaits you. Darkness looms on the horizon, and the forces that seek to harm you are gathering strength. Your journey has only just begun."

Merci listened intently, her heart pounding in her chest. She knew she couldn't afford to falter or succumb to fear. The weight of the world now rested upon her shoulders, and she had to find the strength within to face the encroaching darkness. Merci vowed at that very moment to embrace her heritage, to unlock her hidden powers, and confront the imminent threat that loomed over humanity. Her path was uncertain, but she was no longer alone; Asag, the mysterious entity without form, would be her guide and protect her, preparing her for the battle that was sure to come.

Drifting into a troubled sleep, Merci's dreams were haunted by fragmented visions of ancient battles, celestial beings, and a destiny intertwined with the fate of the world. The threads of her existence were intricately woven, and she held the key to unlocking the ancient mysteries that would shape the course of history. The next chapter in her life was awaited and filled with peril and possibility, and as Merci embraced her ancestral legacy, she knew that she would face the darkness head-on for the survival of humanity and that her own depended upon it.

The death of the entire excavation team was headline News; the strangeness of the whole thing spread around the world. The question was, "What had done this?" not "Who had done this?" By opening the inverted pyramid, they had released onto the world some type of ancient evil. All the world's archaeologists converged on the sight, every news agency, as well as every Ancient Alien theorist.

When word reached New York of the happenings in the Egyptian desert, the detectives immediately went to Cairo because that excavation site was where Merci was supposed to be,, after arriving they along with all the law enforcement agencies began sorting through the dismembered bodies, they found no evidence that Merci was among the dead. So, where was she the detectives were now convinced that in every way all of this revolved around Merci Lowe.

The news reached the heavens of all the chaos on Earth. Anu knew that the Royal heir was at the center of it. Ishtar realized that her prisoner had escaped his prison. Antu was terrified that Merci had been killed because she could not see, nor did she feel her life force. Anu sent for Asag and Erra.

"What day is it?" Merci asked.

Asag replied, "There's no time here, just endless space."

"What is this place?" she asked him.

"It does not exist as you understand time and space; it is the space that was before time; it is void."

"Why are you doing this?"

"Doing what?" he asked.

"Keeping me here," replied Merci.

"As I said before, I am protecting you."

"Yes! I understood that, but what I do not understand is, who or what are you protecting me from?"

"I do not feel your life force should be taken," he answered.

"What do you mean?" she asked, "look, I don't understand any of this, for all I know is that you are the one who attacked me."

"No, it was not I, it was…" she interrupted him before he could finish his comment, "How do I know? I couldn't see him, nor can I see you."

Merci felt that it was time for her to attempt to appeal to whatever this thing was.

As the silence enveloped them, Merci pondered her situation; she couldn't see Asag, the entity who claimed to be protecting her. Attempting to use her intuition, sensing a flicker of compassion in his voice, she knew there was more to this enigmatic being and she needed to unravel the mysteries surrounding her own existence.

"I need to know the truth," she insisted, her voice resolute, "Why am I the one who needs protection? What makes me so special?" Asag's voice carried a weight of ancient wisdom as he responded, "You are the descendant of a great celestial lineage, the bearer of powers bestowed upon you by the blood that flows through you, Your life force. The beings that threaten you seek to exploit those powers for their own nefarious purposes. I am here to ensure that that does not happen."

"Who or what are these forces? What do they want with me? My life force," Merci pressed even harder, her curiosity driving her to uncover the secrets that continue to shroud her identity.

"The fallen ones. They were banished from the heavens; they seek to harness your abilities to unleash chaos upon the world," he explained, "they desire dominion over humanity to reign in darkness and distinguish the light.

Your destiny is intertwined with theirs, as you possess the potential to tip the scales in favor of humanity or their destruction."

Merci's mind grappled with the enormity of the revelation. She always felt a deep connection to the mystical realm, a sense of being part of something greater than herself. Now confronted with the truth, she understood that her existence carried a weighty responsibility.

"I cannot hide forever, Asag," she said with determination burning in her voice, "I must face these forces and fulfill my purpose; I will not allow them to control my fate or that of humanity."

Asag's presence seems to swell with pride. "You possess courage and strength that is truly remarkable, but remember, royal one, the journey ahead is perilous and full of the unknown. The Fallen ones are relentless, and the fate of countless lives will depend on you. Gather allies, unlock the powers within you, and confront the darkness that seeks to consume the world."

Merci nodded, accepting her newfound destiny, knowing the path ahead would be treacherous and filled with unimaginable challenges, and suddenly, feeling an inner turmoil, a burning power waiting to be unleashed.

Now, the void would become home; Merci had to prepare herself to return to the realm of time and space; she had to embrace her role, understanding that she was the Royal heir to the House of The Anunnaki, the one destined to protect humanity from the encroaching darkness.

With Asag's guidance, she will forge her own path and shape the outcome of this ancient battle. The forces of Good and Evil were gathering, and the world awaited its champion. Merci was ready to face the trials head-on, with the knowledge that her journey would define her fate and the future of mankind.

"The danger that you must face comes not from me but from the heavens. How are you feeling?" he asked.

Shouting in the direction of the voice, "How do I feel? I feel like hell; I don't know what's happening to me. I'm sitting here talking to something I can't see. I was almost killed by something I couldn't see. I do not know what has happened to my colleagues, and I don't know where the hell I am, so how does that tell you how I feel? What is that horrible smell? It smells like death," she said.

His reply frightened her, "That's because I am death. Eat and rest," he said, "I will return later with more food and water; until then, you are safe," and then he was gone, and so was the smell. The archaeologist in her made her investigate her surroundings. As she moved around the darkness, she was interrupted only by the fire that was keeping her warm. There were no windows or doors, there was no way out, no way to escape. Thinking to herself, if I could escape, where would I go? There are forces that I do not understand trying to kill me. I need time to understand what and why.

"While figuring out how to save myself and humanity. It looks like Asag is trying to help; still, what is his motivation? What's in it for him? I need answers, and he seems to have them all."

Back on Earth, there was still no sign of Merci, and the detectives were frustrated by that fact. Where was she? Where had she disappeared to? Was she even still alive? Then, out of the corner of his eye, one of the detectives noticed the two men dressed in black again. He began walking towards them, and they began to walk away. The detective asked, "Who are you, and why have I seen you at all my crime scenes?" One of them stopped while the other continued to walk away.

"I am Agent Blake," he said, as he quickly flashed his badge, "We are with Homeland Security."

"Why is Homeland Security interested in a dig site in the middle of the Egyptian desert?"

"The same reason you are," replied Detective Blake, "and why is Homeland Security interested in this crime scene?"

"That is classified information and well above your pay grade." "No disrespect to the job you do, but I'm sure you understand," was his response.

More and more, the detectives were growing increasingly frustrated by Merci's disappearance, as well as the mysterious forces at play. The unexplained deaths and the presence of the Homeland Security agents only deepened their sense of unease; something bigger was happening, something far beyond their comprehension.

While continuing the investigation, the detectives couldn't shake the feeling that they were being watched; every step they took was being monitored. Agent Blake had left them with more questions than answers, and the truth seemed to slip further from their grasp; rumors swirled around the excavation site. Whispers of ancient prophecies and long-forgotten powers.

The darkness that had been unleashed loomed over them like an impenetrable cloud, and the detectives knew they were running out of time. Back at the void, Merci wrestled with her own fears and uncertainties. Asag's cryptic words echoed in her mind. His claim to be death haunted her thoughts. Needing answers and needs to understand her own role in this unfolding battle between light and darkness. What would it take to defeat this demon? The air grew thick with anticipation as her determination swelled within her. She wouldn't let fear hold her back; she would find a way to harness her untapped powers to confront the forces that sought to destroy her and claim dominion over the world.

Meanwhile, the detectives push forward, delving deeper into the mysteries that surround Merci and the inverted pyramid. Tales emerged from ancient texts and long-forgotten legends, painting a picture of an age-old conflict, a cosmic struggle that transcends time itself. As they pieced together the puzzle, a chilling realization dawned upon them: they were not the only ones seeking the truth.

Dark Forces, both human and otherworldly, were closing in. Their intentions were shrouded in malevolence, and with each passing moment, the stakes grew higher. Merci's fate intertwines with the destiny of humanity.

The detectives knew they had to act swiftly, for the battle between light and darkness had not yet reached its climax.

In the depths of the Void and the corridors of their Earthly investigation, the final pieces of the puzzle await their discovery. Secrets long guarded, Powers yet unleashed, and a confrontation that would determine the very fate of existence. The forces of Good and Evil were on a collision course, and Merci stood at its epicenter. Her choices would shape the outcome of this age-old war. The countdown had begun, battle lines had been drawn, and the universe held its collective breath, waiting for the clash that would decide the fate of worlds.

After the confrontation with Homeland Security, the detectives were explaining it to their bosses in New York when one of the Egyptian police beckoned for them to follow him, telling them that they had found a video made by the excavation team. They all watch the tape, including homeland security, finding out that Merci had left the site to go to Babylon, to the gate of the goddess Ishtar, to make certain that her interpretation of the ancient writings were correct. Making them promise not to open the pyramid until she returns.

After she had been gone for a week without any communication, those in charge decided that the archeology department could not financially afford to wait any longer, so they opened the pyramid without her. What happened next, you had to see to believe. As they watched the team crack open the seal, immediately a cloud appeared, and then pure carnage was the aftermath. Bodies flew everywhere, bone-chilling screams filled the air, then a daunting silence took over, and suddenly, a figure appeared before the camera.

Nothing could have ever prepared the room for what they saw next, with all their eyes transfixed on the screen, what appeared look like Satan himself, and it was as if this thing was looking straight at them as if he could see them through the lens of the video camera.

Shock gave way to fear as they all knew at that very moment that hell was upon Earth. It had just gotten very real; everything that they believed and everything that they knew about the world in that single moment had changed. They had all witnessed the coming of the end of days. Still, in the back of the detective's mind, he wondered what all this had to do with Merci, expressing this to his partner, knowing that they needed to find her.

They had someone in NYC check on her and her mother, Dr. Lowe's background. The direction this case was taking was intimidating, knowing that finding Merci was the first step in solving this case because the murders in the United States had taken place before they opened the pyramid.

After the horrifying video revelation, the detectives had a renewed sense of urgency; the image of the figure resembling Satan himself haunted their thoughts, fueling the determination to find Merci and uncover the truth behind these catechistic events. They knew time was running out as chaos gripped the world.

The Worldwide Press and officials across Nations reported unexplained deaths and supernatural occurrences, and these reports flooded in as they delved deeper into the investigation. Encountering resistance and obstruction from those who sought to keep these secrets hidden. Undeterred, the detectives embarked on this race against time, traversing unknown paths to uncover the whereabouts of Merci.

Following her trail to Babylon, the Fable city of ancient Mysteries. The air is thick with tension as they approach the Temple of the goddess Ishtar, where Merci had sought answers. Inside the temple, a sense of foreboding hung heavy in the air. As they cautiously explored its ancient chambers, illuminated only by the flickering of the torchlight, the hieroglyphics, and cuneiform inscriptions seemed to whisper secrets, long forgotten, their meanings hidden to all except those who possess the key.

Suddenly, a sound echoed through the temple, a mix of distant chanting and unearthly roars. They exchanged anxious glances, and with weapons drawn, they pressed forward, their senses heightened, ready to face whatever awaited them. Descending deeper into the Temple's depths, the ground shook beneath their feet, threatening to crumble their resolve.

The confrontation with ancient forces loomed nearer, their power palatable and threatening to consume all in its path. In a chamber veiled in darkness, they searched for Merci, but the forces that they would face were unlike anything they had ever encountered. The air crackled with malevolence.

As the ancient demon Asmodeus materialized before them, his form twisted and contorted, eluding a power that shook the very foundation of their beliefs. With every fiber in their being, the detectives fought back, engaging in a desperate battle for survival. The clash of light against darkness filled the chamber, illuminating the ancient symbols that were scattered around the walls. The supernatural battle raged on, with each side unleashing their most devastating attacks.

The echoes of their struggle reverberated through the temple as if the very foundations of the ancient structure trembled under the weight of their conflict, and in that darkness, a light, a glimmer of hope emerged. As the tide begins to turn, the combined forces of determination and courage push back against the encroaching evil, and victory seems within reach. That flicker of light in the encroaching darkness burned bright, but the battle was far from over.

Asmodeus, wounded but undeterred, unleashed his final onslaught, having not yet regained his full strength and power. Asmodeus was determined to claim victory and plunged the world into eternal darkness. The detectives braced themselves for the ultimate confrontations, aware that, at this moment, the fate of humanity rested on their shoulders.

With every ounce of strength, every shred of conviction, they fought on, determined to prevail against this ancient force that sought to consume them.

In that pivotal moment, the true power of humanity, the power of love, courage, and unwavering belief, is searched for and found. The final crash resonated through the temple, a clash of ancient forces and mortal will. And in that climatic moment, light triumphed over darkness. The ancient demon momentarily vanished, his power extinguished by the unwavering resolve of those who stood against him.

Exhausted but victorious, the detectives emerged from the temple, the weight of the world still on their shoulders, knowing that this battle was not the end and that the forces of darkness were forever seeking to regain their hold on the minds of man. They were prepared to face whatever challenges lay ahead. United in their purpose to protect and preserve the world they held so dear.

Gazing upon the horizon, the sun had begun to rise, casting its warming light upon the earth once more. The darkness had been temporarily pushed back, if only for a while, and with that kind of hope, they embarked on this journey, this journey of understanding and a renewed commitment to safeguarding the delicate balance between light and darkness.

The detectives continued to search tirelessly for Merci, but the efforts seemed in vain. Every lead they pursued turned cold, leaving them with more questions than answers. As time passed, their desperation grew, and they couldn't shake off the lingering sense that something strange was amidst. Unbeknownst to them, Merci was not within their reach. Asag, that veiled being who had saved her, had hidden her away in the depths of the Void, shielding her from the prying eyes of both Heaven and Earth.

In this realm, she existed in a state between worlds, her presence veiled from those who sought to harm her. Asag watched over Merci with a mixture of protectiveness and anticipation. He knew that the forces converging upon the mortal realm would stop at nothing to find her.

In the void, Asag trained her, guided her, and prepared her for the trials that lay ahead. He sensed her innate strength, her untapped potential, and understood that she held the key to a greater destiny. Meanwhile, the detectives, plagued by the inability to locate Merci, dug deeper into the mysteries that had surrounded her.

Then, countless dead ends and deceptions at every turn, their frustration mounted with each passing day. Yet a flicker of determination within them refused to be extinguished; they refused to abandon their quest, compelled by an unyielding belief that finding Merci was paramount to unraveling the mysteries of the world.

As Time stretched on, the forces of darkness grew boulder, wreaking havoc upon the earth. The detectives were violently battling against the encroaching chaos, driven by a relentless pursuit of truth. They understood that without Merci, their chances of deciphering the ancient prophecies and thwarting the impending catastrophe were diminished.

Merci was transforming within the depths of the void. Her encounter with Asag expanded her understanding of the ancient forces at play, revealing the depth of her own power and purpose. She was trying to embrace her role as guardian, a beacon of light against encroaching darkness. As the detectives came closer to uncovering the truths, Asag felt it necessary to reveal himself. Appearing before them, a figure shrouded an enigma, never revealing the whereabouts of Merci, but he did reveal fragments of the intricate web of ancient secrets.

Conveying to them the urgency of their mission and the significance of Merci's role in the battle between the light and the dark. Initially taken aback by Asag's presence and then gradually accepting his guidance while realizing that their paths were intertwined, their shared goal of safeguarding Merci was driving them forward. With a newfound determination, they embarked on a perilous journey into the unknown, guided by this demon's cryptic wisdom.

With joint effort, they began to uncover fragments of ancient prophecies, piercing into the ancient past and putting together the puzzle of the world's fate as their understanding deepened. They became aware of the eminent convergence of celestial forces in a cosmic crash that threatened to unravel the very fabric of the universe itself.

The detectives prepared for the impending battle. Their united purpose, fueled by unwavering results, became an unbreakable bond against the darkness. While still in the void, Merci honed her abilities, embracing her destiny as the protector of humanity.

As the final battle for mankind's survival raged on, the detectives, now with newfound knowledge and forged alliances, stood ready to face the ultimate test with the fate of the world hanging in the balance. They ventured forward, their spirits unyielding and determined to safeguard the fragile equilibrium between light and darkness.

In the void hidden from sight, Merci was trying to embrace her role, channeling her strengthened purpose with Asag by her side, guiding her every step. She would emerge from the depths of the void prepared to confront the forces that threatened to plunge the world into eternal darkness, yet the journey was far from over.

The battle ahead would test her resolve, their alliances, and the very limit of her existence. Separately but together, they stood united, ready to face whatever waited in the land of shadows and to bring the light to the darkness that now reached every corner of the world.

Chapter 11: The Void

Anu paced back and forth in his chamber, deeply troubled by the chaos unleashed upon humanity by Asmodeus. Knowing that only Ishtar possessed the power to subdue the demon and protect the mortal realm, he also felt a sense of urgency to locate the missing royal heir, summoning Ishtar to his chamber and explaining the dire situation.

"We face a grave threat to humanity; Asmodeus is loose and wreaking havoc upon the world. We need your help to find him once again and prevent further destruction."

Ishtar nodded solemnly, aware of her responsibility as a goddess to protect mankind. Yet, unable to shake the feeling that Merci was somehow connected to all of this, deciding to keep her concerns to herself for the time being.

"I will confront Asmodeus and put an end to his rampage," Ishtar replied firmly as she left the Divine chamber. She couldn't help but think about Merci and how her fate was still unknown. Ishtar was heart ached with worry, but she knew she had to focus on the immediate threat and deal with Asmodeus before searching for answers about Merci's whereabouts.

On Earth, the detectives were determined more than ever now to find Merci because they understood her role in the unfolding events; all the clues they had discovered pointed to a larger cosmic plan, one that involved ancient prophecies and the clash of celestial forces.

They couldn't ignore the significance of Merci's existence in the midst of all of this as their investigation intensified, leading them to uncover more hidden truths about the ancient texts and the enigmatic connection between Merci and the impending celestial battle.

The detectives realize that the fate of humanity and the heavens were again inexplicably intertwined. In the void, Merci continued learning, growing stronger and more aware of her potential. Asag had become a mysterious mentor, guiding her through the vastness of the void and helping her to discover the untapped powers within her.

The king's displeasure reverberated through the Grand Halls of the heavens. Frustrated by the lack of progress, he decided to take matters into his own hands; however, his calmness sent shivers down the spines of those around him.

Asag knew he had to act swiftly to protect Merci and evade the King's watchful eye. Asag's thoughts raced back to the conversation with Merci; her plea for guidance had ignited a spark within him. He understood that she needed him in human form to comprehend his instructions fully.

Her skepticism was rooted in the tangible world that she saw with her eyes, not the ethereal realm of sound and energy. So, with his shifting abilities, Asag chose an appearance that would put Merci at ease; long locks framed his sharp features, and his countenance excluded an otherworldly yet captivating allure.

As he approached, her initial fears gave way to a curious apprehension and appreciation of his new presence, and the smell was gone as well. Gently placing a coconut shell filled with the elixir of Life beside her, offering her a taste. The water, drawn from a primordial source, carried the essence of time and existence within its pure droplets. Merci marveled at the taste, a sensation that transcended the boundaries of ordinary water.

Seeking a connection to the temporal realm, Merci inquired about the day, but Asag's response shattered her understanding of time and space; in the void, such concepts don't exist. Merci's upcoming 21st birthday, a significant milestone in her life, was an event destined to be celebrated by the heavens. Asag revealed the truth that had been concealed from her; he spoke of her divine lineage, a

Heritage intertwined with celestial beings. Her blood was infused with the essence of gods, gifting her with extraordinary powers. He guided her through the labyrinth tapestry of her destiny, emphasizing the pivotal role she will play in the cosmic balance.

With patience and wisdom, Asag mentored Merci, nurturing her burgeoning abilities and guiding her through the enigmatic challenges that lay ahead impressing upon her the importance of understanding and controlling her gifts, hinting at a future with choices, and presenting great consequences that would test her resolve.

In the emptiness of the void, Asag's words gave her strength, and a bond formed between them, transcending the boundaries of time and space. She agreed to his guidance, and he vowed to shield and protect her until she was ready to stand on her own.

In the void, an otherworldly connection flourished: a delicate alliance between a mortal with untapped potential and a timeless being with a mysterious purpose. Asag's presence radiated reassurance, and Merci embarked on a journey of self-discovery, her path illuminated by the enigmatic knowledge of the void and the ethereal mentor by her side. The void stretched endlessly, a realm untouched by the constraints of time and space. It was a place where the boundaries of reality blurred into obscurity, and the familiar concepts of day and night, past or future, held no value.

In this surreal expanse, a sensational physical world dissolved, replaced by an eerie tranquility that seemed to emanate through the very fabric of existence itself. Visions of swirling energies dance in the distance, casting hues of azure and Amethyst across the formless expanse. Threads of shimmering light flowed through the void; there was a surreal glow, revealing fleeting glimpses of forgotten truths and hidden knowledge.

There was a sense of mystery as if the very secrets of creation lay just beyond the veil of perception. In this dimensionless realm, sound was but a distant memory and silence prevailed, broken only by the soft echoes like whispers on the wind. The air held the weightlessness that transcended the grasp of gravity, and every moment seemed to defy the laws of physics as if the very rules that govern reality had been rewritten.

Shadows of light intertwined, creating a mesmerizing dance of contrast that seemed to beckon the observer into deeper contemplation. It was a place where truths were revealed and illusions shattered, where the profound and the enigmatic coalesced into a realm beyond imagination.

Yet despite its boundless mysteries and beauty, the void also held an unsettling aura and underlying tension that hinted at forces beyond comprehension. It was a place where destiny and choice converged, where the threads of fate were interwoven with the limitless possibilities of the cosmos. In this timeless sanctuary, Merci found herself both lost as well as found.

A drift in a sea of uncharted potential. The massive void cradled her, its essence becoming a canvas upon which her journey of self-discovery unfolded, guided by the enigmatic presence of Asag, her guardian. Anu's worries deepened as Antu and Ishtar's connection to Merci remained hidden from him. The celestial King knew that the unfolding events were far more complex than even he was yet to understand. His only hope was that Ishtar's intervention would quell the chaos and protect humanity until all could be revealed.

In the heavens and on the earth, the battle for the future had begun. Her body had healed, and a renewed strength coursed through her veins, allowing her to think clearly once more. However, the ache of missing her friends, particularly Adonis, weighed heavily on her heart; she wondered whether he was searching for her and whether he felt the same emptiness that she did.

Thoughts of the pyramids' fate also troubled her, hoping against hope that her colleagues had refrained from opening its forbidden depths. "Asag, I have a question for you. You're a demon, correct?" she inquired. "Yes," he responded simply. "Then why are you helping me?" she wondered, her curiosity brimming. "You are of the utmost importance to the future of the realm," he replied. "Ah, the Anunnaki," she is now connecting the dots. "Why do those who seek my death want me dead?" she further questioned, her voice tingling with frustration.

"You are the rightful heir to the royal bloodline, and there are those who wish to dismantle the power of the Anunnaki Dynasty. The prophecy speaks of your eternal rule, a destiny they aim to prevent," Asag explained.

"Was it you who attacked me at the Temple of Ishtar?" she asked, her brows narrowing. "No, it wasn't my doing, though I was present; seeing you defenseless moved me to intervene," he admitted. "Do you know of Antu and Ishtar?" Merci probed. "Yes, Antu is our Queen, and Ishtar, her sister, the goddess of war," Asag answered, sensing a hidden layer of inquiry beneath her words. "I've been told that Antu is my mother and that the woman I know as Estelle Lowe, my adopted mother, is the goddess Ishtar. Is this true?" she questioned, seeking confirmation. "Yes, your understanding is correct," he affirmed. "So all of this is real?" then she laughed aloud with a mixture of awe and disbelief in her voice. "Indeed, it is, your majesty," Asag confirmed. "Please drop the formal title; just call me Merci." "I prefer not to, Royal one," he remarked with a hint of amusement in this tone.

Their conversation went deeper as Merci brought up her work before the attack, seeking to understand Asag's knowledge. His response revealed an unsettling truth: her colleagues had opened the inverted pyramid, and the consequences were horrific. Asmodeus, one of the rulers of Hell, had been unleashed, resulting in their gruesome demise.

The weight of guilt crushed over her, and tears welled in her eyes. "It's all my fault," she started, being consumed by anguish. Asag's voice was gentle, his reassurance unwavering, "No, Merci, it is not your fault." "But I could have prevented it," her voice choked with emotion. Asag offered her Solace and an explanation, yet a shadow of an untold story lingered, intriguing her further.

"Tell me, Asag," she urged determination in her eyes, "if it wasn't you, then who or what attacked me at the Temple of Ishtar?" Asag hesitated, his voice carrying a weight of secrets yet to be unveiled. "That is a story better left for later," he finally said. Merci's determination flared, a fierce spark in her eyes, "Hell no, it's not; remember, you're talking to a girl from Harlem; you can't just tell me anything." Asag's response carried an air of honesty, "Well, you are not just that; you are the royal heir to the great House of the Anunnaki, the creators of this race of strong, stinking cloud, and most times, ungrateful humans. They created the temple, and The Great I Am gave it life." "By temple, what do you mean?" "The human body is what I mean," responded Asag.

A hint of fire ignited in Merci's gaze, "Watch it, you're talking to one of those stinking humans, and I wouldn't talk about stink if I were you." She laughed. Asag's voice was steady and unwavering, "Yes, but that is not only what you are; that is a very small part of who you are." Her curiosity is unquenched, her tone earnest. "What has mankind done to you to make you hate us so?" Asag's reply held a gravity that settled over the room, "That is not what is important now; what you must do is understand the things that are happening, and you must be ready." "Ready for what?" she injected, her tone a mix of urgency as well as confusion. "Who is after me?" she asked, "You told me why, but you have not told me who? You talk about these powers I've never needed before or knew that I had, so why now? And when I was getting my ass kicked in a temple, where were those so-called powers then? Anyway, I don't even know what these powers are I'm supposed to have?"

His voice resonated with a sense of authority, "You will have command over the heavens and the Earth, over the mind and the body of all living things. That is what is within you. You will possess great strength and wisdom. You will also be remembered for your bravery. You already have the power of life and death. In time, you will be invincible."

A hint of skepticism lingered in Merci's expression, really her tone laced with disbelief, "And when will I wake up from this nightmare? I don't want to be the royal heir to some damn alien throne from God knows where."

Asag's response held back some, but the truth was, "The kingdom of Nibiru is millions of years old. They are a race of warriors who traverse the universe in search of different things. Some scout for planets to inhabit, and others scout for precious metals, mostly gold, which is crucial for their atmosphere." The edge of frustration is shown in Merci's voice. "Why me?" She asked.

Asag responded with conviction, "Because, royal one, it is your destiny."

A strong restlessness gripped her, and her words carried a desperate plea, "I'm feeling like a prisoner. I need to get out of this place. Why are there no doors or windows? Can I at least go outside? I'm going crazy, Asag." "Please!" his response was measured, "I'm not so sure you're ready for that." Her frustration grew, her determination unyielding.

"If you don't get me out of here, I'll find a way out," she declared, her frustration propelling her to make a defiant gesture. He met her challenge head-on, "You are correct; I can feel the anger building up within you. Okay, I have something to show you; come with me."

Asag guided Merci's perception beyond the confines of their chamber, revealing the vast expanse of the universe. Stars glittered in the darkness, and galaxies danced in cosmic harmony. Asag explained, "Here, time has no relevance. The universe is too vast for time to hold any significance." Asag shared the profound complexity of the multiverse, showing her glimpses of her home in different dimensions.

Harlem manifested in the 4th and 5th dimensions, each revealing alternate versions of reality. Sariah, her friend, appeared as a mayor in one dimension and a jewel thief in another. Fatima's destiny diverged from one as a world-famous dancer to the other being cut short by influenza.

"I've seen all the lives that my friends have led in other dimensions; the only thing I do not see is me. Why is that, Asag?" Merci asked, her curiosity driving her deeper. Asag recognized her insight and her willingness to question and seek answers. It was a pivotal moment, a test that she had passed. Yet he chose his words carefully, "It seems you have a keen perception, royal one." As Merci's understanding grew, so did her inquiries. She gazed upon the heavens, the cosmic tapestry stretching beyond imagination. Asag shared the secrets of the constellations, the mysteries of distant galaxies, and the enigmatic city of the Gods within a constellation. His voice carried the weight of ancient knowledge. "The years of Earth have been many, but the days of Man on it are few. More than half a millennium ago, a vibrant human civilization thrived there, only to be wiped out and the Earth cleansed. A cycle attributed to Enlil."

"The Earth cleansed?" Merci asked in disbelief. "Yes," Asag confirmed, "The Enlil cycle has repeated itself countless times. Mankind's history is a mere fragment." He taught her all about the universe's tapestry. Asag's guidance expanded her perception, unveiling the celestial wonders of Andromeda, The star of Enlil, and the City of the Gods. He illuminated the history of mankind on Earth, revealing cycles of them rising and then their Falls, spanning Millions of millennia.

Back in the realm of the Gods, anxiety rippled through the divinity as they grappled with uncertainty and the absence of Merci; Antu's concern weighed heavily. Her connection with Merci's life force is disrupted, leaving her restless and vulnerable to doubt. "Where is she?" Antu's voice trembled, her anxiety evident. Ninhursag tried to ensure her, offering an explanation and reasoning. Yet the unease persisted as if the very fabric of existence was fraying at the edges.

The chambers of power were a sanctuary of tension. Enlil approached his father, his cautious footsteps echoing a sense of foreboding; he was met with a chilling atmosphere—a harbinger of unsettling events to come. "Father," Enlil called out, his voice respectful yet laced with concern. He stepped forward, approaching the king's chamber with caution, well aware that the tides of fate were shifting, and an ominous storm loomed on the horizon.

The room seemed to hold its breath, with a heavy silence punctuated by the weight of impending darkness. The exchange between Father and Son remains cloaked in uncertainty, mirroring the temperature of their predicament. "Father, may I enter?" Enlil questioned before entering his father's room. "I'd like to talk to you about the carnage on Earth and the Kingdom." The feeling of his father's dissatisfaction rests heavily on his shoulders. "May I speak freely?" he asked. "Yes," replied Anu, short and calm. "Maybe you should not stop Asmodeus?"

"Why?" said his father.

"Because humans have become a threat to the planet and to us. They are currently in the fourth stage of Kaluga; for them, this is a time of strife, and evil roams the planet. There are those within the kingdom who feel your love for mankind does not allow you to see the flaws in them. This, my king, is what causes the upheaval we currently face, and this has added to the conflict among your people."

Enlil knew just how to get his father's focus off of the royal heir; all he had to do was distract his father by returning his mind to the ruling of the Kingdom. Enlil felt that he could do a better job, much better than his father. He would soon get the chance to prove it. The king was well aware of the troubles in his kingdom, knowing that his attention had not been on ruling the kingdom as much as it had been on finding the royal heir.

"Father," said Enlil, "I will find the Royal heir for you." Still, he could see the distress in his father's energy field. The king tried hard not to show it. But Enlil knew which of the royal females had birthed the heir; he'd found the answer during work on the Royal DNA column. Checking all the royal females against the heir's DNA, and there it was. It had been right in front of him all the whole time. This information he would use when the time was right

In quiet contemplation, the king reflected on what Enlil had spoken, and he was correct; this was a time of strife, and Evil was running rampant on the Earth. Everything that mankind is currently facing is his own doing, but Enlil was wrong in that Anu did not see their flaws because he did. "When Yahweh said let us make man in our image, "we did," then he sent His son to die for the past and the future sins of the world, and even with all that, they have forgotten us. These humans have no respectful life or the world they have been given, so I do understand Enlil's disdain for them. They have forgotten the old ways; they now worship things and each other. To this generation of this species, we are just myths and legends. We, the gods of the sky, have always assisted and influenced mankind, but we cannot alter their path. They are writing their own story. The opening of The Pyramid was their own doing. Still, I have sent Ishtar to attempt to re-imprison Asmodeus, and for their sake, I hope she's up to the task because their lack of belief in us has weakened our power over them."

Enlil was certain his plan was coming together. I must find the Royal heir first; he thought to himself. He knew exactly who to get that information from. Heading for the Queen's chamber, Enlil saw Enki leaving the queen's chamber, speaking as they passed each other, wondering what the other was up to.

Enlil noticed that his mother had not had much interest in things scientific lately; she was preoccupied with something. They were up to something, and he planned on finding out exactly what it was. He was sure that it had something to do with the royal heir.

When the detectives reached New York, the city was cloaked in an unsettling calm, an eerie contrast to its usual hustle and bustle. The detectives experienced a gaze scanned the horizon, sensing an impending storm, not a river, but of a darker nature. It was as if the very air whispered of an approaching reckoning, a presence that weighed heavily on his shoulders; his determination unyielding, he set his sights on unraveling the Enigma surrounding the lows.

Their home in Harlem became his starting point, a potential portal into the heart of this perplexing case. Conversations with neighbors and acquaintances offered fragmented insights and snippets of a life lived amidst ancient mysteries.

The detectives traced the thread of their existence to a five-story walk-up they called home. The property management company provided a paper trail that led to Dr. Lowe's old attorney. Yet the information was unveiled. It was a landscape of business dealings and financial transactions, a stark contrast to the personal details he sought. Within the web of legalities and assets, one truth emerged: Merci Lowe, the enigmatic heiress, possessed substantial wealth, yet her financial interactions had stilled. Credit cards lay dormant, and all communication had ceased as if the world had lost touch with her.

The lawyer's recollection painted a picture of a woman who had embarked on a journey to Egypt only to disappear into obscurity. Back at his office, the detective turned to the digital realm. Googling the name Dr. Estelle Lowe, the computer screen displayed a mosaic of an Archaeologist, archaeological triumphs—a tapestry woven with images of her among historical discoveries.

It was a life marked by exploration and an existence rich with travel and revelation. Page 60, a digital time capsule from 1912, revealed a photograph that had been frozen in time, a glimpse into an excavation that unveiled the Nefertiti bust, and an icon from the lost city of Akhenaten. Among the figures in the photograph stood Dr. Estelle Lowe, a consultant in that distant time and space, another age in mankind's evolution.

Strangely, as he compared the photo to the more recent images of Dr. Lowe, a disturbing truth emerged: her appearance had defied time itself. The detective's voice sliced through the air, "Who is this woman?" In pursuit of answers, his keystrokes led him deeper into the Labyrinth of records. A search for Esther Aristarr Lowe's birth certificate, a seemingly mundane document that held the promise of untold secrets. A trail leading to nowhere.

As his detective brain dove into the digital recesses, shadows danced. Beyond his window, the city's pulse quickened with an ominous undercurrent. Unbeknownst to him, his pursuit of truth had ignited ripples that would reach far beyond the realm of a mere investigation into the realms of destiny and the cosmic unknown.

As he began an endless search for Dr. Lowe's birth record, the digital archives began to shift, and the annals of history blurred. To his astonishment again, the detective's efforts bore no fruit, no trace of her birth in any century, as if she emerged from the shadows of time itself. The implications were staggering, leaving him standing on the precipice of a cosmic mystery.

Piecing together the puzzle, a surreal tapestry emerged before him. A woman, seemingly untouched by the ravages of age, a century-old Enigma shrouded in youth. A baby found within an archaeological embrace, devoid of birth parents or origin. Adopted by the illustrious Dr. Lowe. Now, a journey to the heart of Egypt leads to a perilous and subsequent vanishing.

His laughter echoed through the solitude of his workspace, still laced with the threat of irony, the absurdity of this situation, and the convergence of the uncanny. The impossible seemed almost poetic, retirement beckoned on the horizon, a siren's call. He half-jokingly vowed to heed once this enigmatic saga reached its conclusion.

Eager for a new revelation, he delved further and further down this rabbit hole, unraveling the narrative, a thread, one that had woven itself into what was Merci's life. He learned of a mysterious exchange, a child delivered to Dr. Lowe at a dig site by an elusive woman, her identity a mystery. The child's adoption, her journey to American soil, was a tale painted in broad strokes of intrigue and obscurity.

Yet the detectives hungered for more. To pierce the shrouds of the past and illuminate the shadows that clung to Merci's origin. Placing a call to Dr. Azizi, a name that had been etched into the detective quest. Though the doctor himself remained elusive, the promise of insight hung in the air, awaiting its time to unfold. 18 months had gone by since Adonis' tragic death, the veil of uncertainty weighing heavily upon the detective's shoulders. A single thread of hope remained, a connection to the Enigma that was Fatima Fisher.

As the hospital corridors carried them to her bedside, anticipation, entwined with urgency, was prevalent. Before a single word could pass from the detective's lips, Fatima's voice pierced the silence, recounting the chilling event of that fateful night. A benevolent presence, an otherworldly stench, a force that toyed with life itself, her words painted a canvas of horror, and disbelief reverberated.

As she spoke, a disconcerting question emerged, one that clouded the detective's thoughts, who had placed Adonis' organs beside his lifeless body.

Remembering what they had witnessed in the annals of The Egyptian desert, the detective's mind turned, suspicions spiraling as he went deeper into the abyss of this inexplicable web. As Fatima recounted the incident, tears flowing from her eyes, the room seemed to hold its breath on the precipice of revelation while teetering on the edge of darkness and truth.

The air was solemn, and it hung over the makeshift memorial that adorned her neighborhood. Today was Merci's 21st birthday. As Sky carefully places the vase of flowers, her eyes reflect the collective worry and longing of their friend. Sariah's voice cut through the heavy atmosphere, a mix of reflection and frustration. Wondering if Merci was alive or even aware of Adonis' tragic death. Sariah let out a sigh as she adjusted Merci's picture, the visual embodiment of their unanswered questions.

During the tributes, a sudden jolt of disbelief electrified the group. As a cab pulled to and Halt, and from it, emerged a figure that seemed to defy reality. *Was it her? Dr. Estelle Lowe or her identical twin.* While exiting the cab, Ishtar could hear the questions in everyone's mind, casting aside their uncertainty. The shock now faded, replaced by curiosity and a flood of questions.

Ishtar had returned, assuming the identity of a non-existent twin, to navigate the world she and Merci had inhabited. It was the most seamless way to intertwine herself with her surroundings, as well as to reoccupy the home she and Merci had shared. Her purpose stretched beyond mere reintegration along with her expertise in demonology; she sensed the malevolent currents of Asmodeus' influence sneaking through the world. It was a dark tide marked by increased satanic and occult activities, ritualistic murders, and a horrifying rise in missing children.

Ishtar recognized the signs: humanity was spiraling into chaos, and internal forces were exploiting its vulnerability. Asmodeus coveted the key that Jesus Christ had taken before His ascension to heaven, seeking to reopen the portal to hell. Ishtar knew of the cataclysmic consequences such an act would unleash upon the earth.

Determined to end this impending doom, she vowed to locate the keys before Asmodeus could. Stepping into her old apartment, Ishtar's senses absorbed the residual echoes of a tragedy. Adonis' presence seemed etched into the space, a haunting reminder of the violence that had transpired there.

While having a conversation with the young men and Merci's friends, fragments began to unravel of the story of Fatima's survival, her subsequent confinement in a mental institution, and the residue of Adonis' creativity left behind—his studio equipment. Ishtar's resolve surged. Her purpose crystallized. Needing to piece together the fragments of this grim puzzle, and to find Merci, knowing that she still had to halt the insidious mechanisms of Asmodeus.

With the studio equipment gifted to the young men as both a token of gratitude and a step forward. Ishtar embarked on her mission, infusing her own strength with the determination of Merci's friends.

In the midst of encroaching darkness, the desperate threads of destiny were weaving a tapestry of redemption, courage, and the unfolding pursuit of truth. With curiosity burning, Ishtar asked about her research and personal belongings. The young men, ever helpful, shared that it had all been placed in storage. One of them had the key to that storage unit, having aided Adonis in relocating the items before his death.

The address was promptly provided, and Ishtar was soon able to retrieve her belongings. As she sorted through the remains of her past life, one of many she had experienced, the equipment Adonis had gathered for his studio remained a testament to his aspirations. A gift that Ishtar then bestowed upon his friends.

As the story continued to unfold, the threads of fate and destiny interwoven as Ishtar's quest for answers propelled her forward. Erra had picked up the scent of humans on Asag the last time he'd seen him but had not been able to stay on his trail because Asag knew he was suspicious.

"Royal one, you have learned well. The time will come very soon for you to take your place in the Royal House of Anunnaki. War on Nibiru is imminent; you must get control over your kingdom and its people before it's too late," said Asag.

"As I told you before, I don't want to rule no damn Kingdom; I just want to go home to my friends," said Merci.

"Well, that is not possible, Royal one, for the world you left behind is no more."

"What do you mean?" she asked.

"When your colleagues opened the pyramid, they Unleashed hell on Earth," he responded.

"The Earth you knew no longer exists. But if mankind is to survive, you must be the one to save them."

"Save them? Oh, so now I'm supposed to save the world. " she said, fighting what she knew deep inside was her destiny.

Before Merci's friends left, they gave Ishtar the business
card with the name and number of the lead detective who
was handling Adonis' murder case. He was also handling
the case of the missing person, which was filed on behalf of
Merci. Since Dr. Esther Lowe was the next of Kin, she'd go
see him and find out any information that he may have.
Heading straight for the front desk and knowing every eye
was on her, Ishtar asked for Detective Black. The officer at
the front desk could not take his eyes off of her, for her
beauty was above any on Earth.

Once the officer got hold of himself, he called for Detective
Black, telling him that Dr. Lowe was at the front desk; still,
he couldn't stop staring at this beautiful woman. The look
on Detective Black's face said it all; it was a combination of
shock, confusion, and awe. Ishtar stepped forward and
introduced herself, "Hello, Detective Black, I'm Dr. Esther
Lowe. Estelle Lowe was my twin sister," reaching out her
hand to shake his, knowing very well that when she
touched him, he was all hers. Instead, he just turned around
and said, "Follow me." *This one,* she thought, *would not be
so easy.* He led her to a corner room with gray walls and a
desk overflowing with files. He had books on the occult
and demons everywhere.

"What can I do for you, Dr. Lowe?" he said, still amazed at how much she resembled her late sister, wondering what kind of bloodline would allow a woman at her age to be this flawless. "Before you answer, Dr. Lowe, I just have one question for my records, you understand."

"Sure, ask away," she responded.

"When and where were you and your sister born?" said the detective, "I can find no record of your birth."

"My sister and I were born on July 18th, 1961; we've never had birth certificates because it was never officially recorded." Detective Black nodded as he jotted down the information, his curiosity evident. Ishtar watched him carefully, assessing his reactions and looking for any sign of suspicion or disbelief.

"I'm sorry for your loss," the detective's demeanor softened. Dr. Lowe was a respected figure in her field; her contributions to archeology were remarkable. "Thank you," Ishtar replied, her tone carrying a mix of appreciation and sadness. "I'm here to gather any information you might have about my sister's daughter, Merci, and also the case of the young man named Adonis Richardson. I understand he was Merci's boyfriend, and he was murdered around the same time that my niece disappeared."

The detective's expression grew more solemn, "Yes, that's correct, Adonis Richardson was tragically murdered in his apartment. It was a brutal and disturbing crime. We're still investigating the case, but we've hit a lot of dead ends."

Ishtar's eyes showed a flicker of concern, "What about my niece's case? Has there been any progress?" Detective Black sighed and leaned back in his chair. "I wish I had better news for you, Dr. Lowe. We've been searching for your niece, but it is as if she's vanished into thin air; no one has seen or heard from her since the day she went on that lone expedition to The Temple of The Goddess Ishtar."

"What do you mean? I thought she disappeared from the site of the Pyramid expedition," said Ishtar.

"No," said Detective Black, "she wanted to confirm what the seal on the pyramid said, and that led her to the temple."

Ishtar's silence made Detective Black a little uneasy; it was as if she knew something, but he wasn't sure. Ishtar's heart dropped, but she remained composed.

"Is there anything you could share about the circumstances of her disappearance? Any leads, any unusual details that might help me understand what's happening." Detective

Black hesitated, studying Ishtar's face; he wasn't used to dealing with family members who looked like her, who exuded an air of mystery.

"Well, it's a puzzling case. Your niece was on an expedition into the Egyptian desert with a team of archaeologists. They were searching for something significant, but we're not exactly sure what. We believe it was the entrance that they were searching for. But what found them is what we don't understand. None of them survived, and there's no trace of your niece."

So, you have no leads on her whereabouts?"

The detective shook his head, "none," he replied as if she had vanished. "We've interviewed the remaining team members who didn't go to the expedition site, and they're just as baffled as we are. It's like something out of a supernatural horror novel."

As Ishtar's mind raced, pieces of the puzzle began coming together. "Is there any chance I can speak to any of those team members?" she questioned, "Perhaps they might remember something that could shed light on what happened."

"I may be able to arrange that," he replied, "they have recently returned from Egypt. They might be able to provide you with more insight. We're open to any ideas or leads or information."

At this point, Ishtar's resolve was growing stronger. She knew she was getting closer to uncovering the truth behind the tangled web of mysteries that surrounded Merci's disappearance. Although she also knew Anu had sent the Hallaku demons and the Sebittu looking for Merci, and she knew that Adonis Richardson's death was their work, she still didn't share that information with Detective Black.

With each piece of information she gathered, the intricate thread of Merci's fate still had not yet become clear. Detective Black sighed; frustration evident in his expression. He hesitated, his eyes flickering with uncertainty. "There have been some strange occurrences and unexplained phenomena surrounding both cases," he reflected, "It is as if there's a darkness that has enveloped them, something beyond the ordinary."

Ishtar connected the dots between the inverted pyramid, the ancient artifacts, and her temple, all a part of the Hidden world of demons and gods. "Detective Black, I understand that this might sound far-fetched, but have you considered the possibility of Supernatural involvement? Demons, perhaps?"

"Have I considered it? My partner and I have confronted it." "Really?" she asked, "When and where did this occur?" Ishtar's curiosity needed answers; now, her Temple was an important part of the puzzle as Detective Black explained the confrontation with Asmodeus and the appearance of the entity who explained a lot of the missing pieces.

Detective Black's eyes watched as he told her of the life-and-death struggle he and his partner had faced in the temple. He was looking for any sign that she knew more than she was letting on, but there was no surprise evident in her expression.

"Supernatural?"

"Yes, I'd say so, and if the truth be told, some of my colleagues have been discussing strange patterns and symbols tied to many of the cases throughout the world. We've been trying to make sense of it all. We have come to the conclusion that we're dealing with something beyond our understanding."

Ishtar's heart was pounding, knowing that she was onto something. "Detective Black, I've done extensive research into ancient artifacts, Myths, and legends. I believe there's a connection here, something that ties into a hidden world that most people aren't aware of. I like to help uncover the truth, find my niece, and bring justice to Adonis Richardson."

Detective Black studied her, his skepticism warring with his curiosity. "Dr. Lowe, I'm willing to explore any and all avenues at this point. If you have information or insights that could help us, I'm all ears."

Ishtar realized that she had found an ally, unwilling or not, in Detective Black. She had a unique perspective, one that merged the world of the supernatural with the realm of humans. Together, they could uncover the mysteries that had eluded them both. As the conversation continued, Detective black asked Ishtar about her and her twin sister Estelle's parents.

"Well," she said, "we never knew our parents. They died in an auto accident when we were babies; we were raised by the sisters in the Church of the Risen Christ in Ethiopia. It burnt down many years ago, so therefore, all our records have been destroyed."

Noticing that while she was talking, the detective was searching through his files. He then placed a copy of a picture on the desk in front of her, and as he pointed to the woman, he asked, "Who's this? This picture was taken over 100 years ago, during the unearthing of the Nefertiti bust, and this article gives the name of the woman as Dr. Estelle Lowe. Now, if you and your sister were born in 1961, how was this picture even possible?"

Ishtar again reached across the table to touch his hand, and again, he avoided her touch. "Well, Detective Black, as I said, my reason for coming to see you is to find out how things were progressing with both of your investigations. I understand that you went to the excavation site in Egypt and that you saw a video of something no one wants to admit that they saw, am I correct?" she said.

"What?" he said, "how do you know that? We were all sworn to silence on that matter; that info was not supposed to leave that room."

"Well, sir, demonology is my field of study. The inverted pyramid has always been part of ancient folklore but finding that it really does exist just makes me want to know more. I'm sure that you know money talks. There are no secrets when money exchanges hands. Besides, you told me of you and your partner's encounter with that same entity."

"Sorry, Dr. Lowe, that information is classified, and you do not have the clearance."

She knew that getting clearance would not be a problem. Just then, the chief commander entered the office to ask Detective Black about the case. Here was that opportunity, this was the opportunity she needed, so she introduced herself with a handshake, explaining to the captain that she was also an archaeologist like her sister, but her field of study was demonology, and that she would gladly offer her services to help in any way that she could. She was granted clearance right then, and there, she would be a consultant on the case.

Detective Black was stunned and a little perturbed at her for inserting herself into his investigation, but the commander made her the Department's Authority on all things occultic. Once the commander had left the room, the detective said in no uncertain terms that he really had no need for her help. But now that she had the proper clearance and was currently the department specialist on demons, he had little choice but to cooperate.

Deep down, he couldn't deny that there was something otherworldly about the cases, and if Dr. Esther Lowe had expertise in this area, it might be their best chance to unravel these mysteries. Detective Black decided to share some of the details that had baffled him and his team. He showed her a video recording from the Egyptian excavation site where strange symbols dotted the landscape. This video captured the chaotic scene with the archaeologists all clearly excited by what they were witnessing.

Ishtar watched the footage, her mind concentrating on the symbols. She explained each one to him, also explaining their ancient ties to demonology and dark rituals. "It's clear that something benevolent was awakened at this site," she said, and she knew exactly what it was. Detective Black nodded, then he said, "We suspected as much, but no one wanted to admit it. We need answers, Dr. Lowe, and we need to find your niece."

"I'll do my best to help Detective because I also need to find my niece, and I believe that these cases are connected. With heightened senses, she knew darkness was growing in this world, one that threatened to consume everything. As they delve deeper into the investigation, they form an uneasy alliance, their path intertwined by the supernatural forces at play. They would need all the knowledge and courage they could muster to face this darkness that was now lurking in the shadows.

Days turned into weeks as Ishtar and Detective Black tirelessly pursued leads, analyzed evidence, and consulted with experts in various fields. The cases seemed to intertwine more with each passing day, revealing a complex web of connections that reached far beyond the mundane world.

Ishtar/Dr. Lowe's knowledge of demonology was invaluable; she deciphered ancient texts, identified symbols, and connected the dots between seemingly unrelated incidents; it became clear that the unearthed pyramid had opened a gateway to a realm of darkness, allowing them to seep into the human world.

One evening, as Ishtar reviewed some of her old research notes, she stumbled upon a hidden compartment in a book. Inside, she found a journal belonging to Merci. The entries were cryptic, describing strange visions, powerful dreams, and a growing sense of fear. Reading between the lines, she could feel it was something that Merci was being pulled towards, something far beyond her control. Meanwhile, Detective Black had traced a series of ritualistic killings that spanned the globe. Each murder seems to be tied to the spread of occult practices, along with the increasing influence of benevolent entities.

The more they learned, the clearer it became that stopping these dark forces was paramount. Their collaboration faced challenges and skepticism from within the police department. Some dismissed their findings as mere superstition, while others feared the consequences of confronting Supernatural entities. But their unwavering determination and Detective Black's growing belief in the extraordinary propelled them forward.

As they uncovered more about the origins of the pyramid and the entities unleashed, realizing that the only way to close the Gateway and prevent a catastrophe was to find the missing key, Ishtar's knowledge of ancient folklore pointed to a remote location where the key might be hidden—a location fraught with danger and dark magic. With a mixture of apprehension, Detective Black's partner and his team embarked on a journey prepared to face the unknown and battle the benevolent forces that threatened humanity's very existence.

As Ishtar and Detective Black ventured deeper into the realm of demons and dark rituals, their alliance strengthened, and they became determined to protect the world from the impending apocalypse.

Now, Ishtar's focus was on reimprisoning Asmodeus. Her mind was mostly on Merci. *Where could she be? Why couldn't she feel her life force?* Not wanting to believe that she had lost her darling Merci.

Chapter 13: The New Earth

Detective Black's eyebrows raised. "What are you doing?" he asked while watching over Ishtar's shoulder, "have you found something?"

With a calm demeanor, Ishtar responded, "No, I haven't found anything concrete. However, I did notice a particular pattern: most of your victims are concentrated within the same area, and they are mostly within the same age range."

His interest peaked as he inquired, "So what does that imply?"

"It suggests that your killer or killers are likely from that very area," she explained.

"There has been a notable increase in occult activities around there recently," he confirmed.

"Do you have any reliable informants within that area?" she pressed.

"I do," he answered.

"Then what are we waiting for? Let's tap into their knowledge and see if they picked up on anything," she urged.

As they made their way through the city, Detective Black switched gears, questioning her, "So you're not curious about the contents of the video I saw in Egypt?"

A hint of a knowing smile played on her lips, "Detective Black, I'm well aware of what you saw."

His surprise was evident, "Really, how?"

"Indeed," she replied, her tone confident, "you witnessed the demon, Asmodeus. He was imprisoned in that pyramid by the goddess Ishtar thousands of years ago. He's known as the ruler of the seventh level of hell, a fact chronicled in ancient tales. The opening of that seal on the pyramid by the archaeologist set in motion the unraveling of this era on earth—the end of days. Asmodeus is the catalyst behind the surge of demon activities, not only in your city but across the entire world."

Detective Black's curiosity is undeniable, "What do you mean by the end times on Earth?"

Ishtar paused for a moment before explaining, "Asmodeus and his Legion are in pursuit of that key to the Gates of Hell. The keys your partner and his team now search for. If he manages to obtain them, it will herald the end times of your world."

The detective, struck by her choice of words, questioned again, "Why do you keep referring to it as your world as if it's not yours also?"

"Can you forgive my phrasing? My words sometimes betray my true feelings."

Silence envelops the car for the remainder of the ride. Ishtar stared out of the window, her thoughts consumed by the mystery of Merci's absence; she couldn't feel Merci's life force, and it troubled her deeply. Ishtar knew that Asmodeus was not responsible for Adonis and Mary Ellen's boyfriend's death; these killings were different. The manner of death and the arrangement of the organs next to the bodies. They bore the hallmarks of the Hallaku and the Sebittu.

Then, like a bolt of realization, it hit her. Perhaps it was Hallaku or the Sebittu who had taken Merci. As they drove through the city, Ishtar sensed death prowling the streets of New York like a stealthy thief snatching souls along its path.

In the otherworldly realm, Merci couldn't hold back her curiosity. "Asag, can I ask you something?"

"Anything you ask, it is my honor to answer," he replied. Hesitating before continuing, Merci asked him, "Why don't I feel anything? Anything significant, I mean?"

Asag understood her concern but questioned, "What do you mean, anything like what?"

"Well, Merci began, "If I possess all this power, why don't I feel it? Why don't I feel any different?"

Asag replied, "Your power flows through your veins; it is in your bloodline, in your DNA. You have not fully undergone your transformation yet." Eager for answers, Merci asked, "So when will that happen?" Asag hesitated, not entirely willing to share the truth just yet. "Soon," was all he said. Asag hesitated, his reluctance evident as he grappled with the information he had to share. He wasn't ready to divulge the entirety of what needed to occur for her complete transformation.

"Do you have any knowledge of your birth? Do you know where you were born?" Asag inquired. Merci pondered the question for a moment. "I think somewhere in the Middle East," she replied, her tone uncertain, "Why do you ask?'

"Can you recall the year of your birth?" Asag continued.

"Of course, I can. I was born in 1991. Today is my 21st birthday," she answered confidently. Asag's response was swift but unexpected, "You are not correct. The place and time of your birth are not as you know them."

Confusion set in as Merci asked, "What do you mean, Asag?"

He continued, "You were born in the ancient city of Nippur." Merci's eyes were a vision of disbelief, "Do you mean ancient Sumerian?"

Asag affirmed, "Yes, precisely."

"That's impossible," Merci said, grappling with the implications. Asag's tone remained patient, "With all that I have taught you and all that you have seen, is anything truly impossible?"

Her skepticism wavered, "I guess not when you put it that way. So, when was I truly born, considering I'm not 21 in ancient times? Am I even really 21?" Merci questioned; her foundation shaken by this revelation.

"In the year 5000 BC. is when you were born," Asag replied, "this is a fact." Merci's eyes widened, her mind racing to comprehend this monumental revelation. "Stop playing with me, Asag," she said. "I do not play; I'm a demon," he stated. His response prompted a reluctant chuckle from Merci. "Well, you have a point there," she laughed.

As the weight of the truth sunk in, Merci finally spoke up again, "So how was I brought into the future?" Asag's gaze held a deep intensity, "Your mother took you into the future and entrusted you to her sister, the goddess Ishtar, who you knew as Estelle Lowe."

Merci stood in stone silence for a moment, her mind grappling with the enormity of what she had just learned. Finally finding her voice, barely a whisper, "How?" Standing there for a moment, she asked, "So, how old am I really?"

"7,012 human years," he replied. "Damn," she said as she walked away. Asag could tell she was really confused. It felt strange learning that she was born in another time and place. "So, when I was born, this world was young, and Mankind was in its infancy?" "Yes," he replied. As an archaeologist, she was aware of the ancient Sumerian civilization and its culture.

As a child, she spent many years there. She had been to many of its city ruins with Estelle; now, things were making sense. That was why Estelle made her learn cuneiform and why Merci felt as if she had been there before. Now, it turned out that she had been.

"Does that time and place still exist?" she asked.

"Yes, it does," he said, "on another plane in another dimension."

"Can I go there?" Merci asked.

"It is not impossible; you would have to go through a time portal into the past."

"Let's go then," she said.

"Not so fast," he said, "We still have work to do."

Merci wanted to experience the Sumerian culture; it was the place of her birth. Wanting to know more, to understand who it was that was born there more than 5,000 years ago. Just then, she got a flashback of the time she was unconscious at the bottom of the tunnel. She told Asag of her walk through the streets of Ur, describing the magnificence of the temples. Telling him of the meeting she had with the queen named Pue-obe. Asag listened intensely, his features inscrutable as he absorbed the details of her experiences. When she finished, he remained silent for a moment before responding.

"Your memories are fragments of a life that spans centuries, Royal one. You were born of a lineage intertwined with both the human and the Divine realms," Asag finally stated. This piqued her curiosity even further. "Tell me more, Asag, about my past, my true origins."

Asag seems distant, lost in the occurrence of time. "Long before your birth in Sumerian, your mother is the powerful Queen and High Priestess. She is the guardian of ancient knowledge. She also possessed the ability to traverse different realms and times. A gift that only a few possess. One which you also possess. Seeing the coming darkness and the rise of Asmodeus along with the impending chaos that he would unleash upon the Earth, she knew that mankind would someday need you, her gift to them. Her eyes darkened as his words began to settle in.

"My mother sent me to the Future to hide me?" she replied, a mix of shock and realization surging through her.

"Yes, Royal One, your birth is considered an abomination, a secret that could disrupt the delicate balance of power in the ancient world. Your mother, torn between her love for you and her duty, made the difficult decision to send you to a time where you could thrive and grow.

Merci's head swirled with conflicting emotions. Always having felt a void, an unexplained longing. Now, she understood that it was tied to her mysterious origins.

"What about my father? Who is he?" she questioned.

Asag's expression turned sympathetic. "Your father is not currently known to me." Although he already knew the truth, he knew of Antu's indiscretion; still, that was something he would never tell Merci or anyone else for that fact.

Asag's gaze darkens.

"Why now?" Merci asked, "Why has this darkness, this Asmodeus, risen to power?"

"He has been a malevolent force throughout history, seeking to break the boundaries between realms and unleash chaos. He senses the potential within you," explained Asag, "the potential to challenge him and his reign of Terror. With the opening of the Pyramid, he saw an opportunity to return to Earth and claim his dominion."

Asag's lips curved with a faint smile, "Your courage and determination are commendable, Royal one, but remember your journey will not be easy. You must embrace your past, your abilities, and the allegiances that will aid you in this battle."

Merci's tenacity is not wavering, "I'm ready to face whatever challenges that come my way, and I won't forget the sacrifice my mother made to protect me." With a newfound understanding and determination, Merci went deeper into her past. Honing her powers and forging allegiances with both morals and beings of other realms. As she navigated through time and dimensions, she embraced her destiny as a Warrior against Darkness, with the legacy of strength to shape the fate of the Cosmo's and humanity.

Asag was not surprised at all. Of this, he was sure. That this was not a dream; her description of the ancient city was in such detail. He knew she had been there.

"Royal one, you thought you were dreaming on that faith-filled day. What really happened is that you astrally projected yourself to that place and time."

Realizing that is where he first tracked her scent. "Your powers have been within you since your birth. My job has been to teach you how to control them.

They have always been there. If I allow you to go there, you will risk discovery, for in that time, the gods walked with mankind."

"That's a chance I'm willing to take," said Merci with a determination that made Asag smile.

"Yes, I'm sure you are. Still, you must remember I was not the only one sent after you," Asag warned.

"I cannot hide here forever, my friend," Merci replied.

"This is true, royal one, but on this journey, I cannot go; you must do this alone. If we were discovered, I could be of no help to you. They would know that it was me who hid you, and if that were to happen, I could no longer be of any assistance to you," Asag explained. He knew that it was time to see what Merci had learned, and he had to let her go.

Reminding her that extended use of her powers would weaken her until she had fully transformed.

"Don't worry, Asag," she said confidently, "I'll be careful." Merci's ability to move through time and space filled her with wonder and excitement. The fact that she could transform into anything or anyone she desired exhilarated her. It was like unlocking a door to endless possibilities like a child in a candy store; Merci looked forward to this adventure. While preparing herself for the journey, she felt a bit of anticipation and curiosity. This was her chance to step into the past to uncover the secrets of her own birth and explore a world where gods and mortals coexisted.

With every fiber of her being, she was now ready to embrace the challenges and the revelations that awaited her. *She would be in and out before anyone noticed,* so she thought.

Chapter 14: Child of The Cosmos

Merci thought this trip would be an easy one, but unknown to her, it would be anything but that. Erra felt that he had failed his King, and for him, this was the first time such a thing had ever happened. He was not going to be made a fool of by anyone, especially a human.

The thought that Asag had betrayed him angered him even more, and he swore to find them both. Erra decided to keep an eye on the Stargate at Ur; this was the first place where he had detected a trace of the royal heir. His instincts told him that it was as good a place as any to watch; if she had been there before, she would likely return.

The Stargate at Ur was one of the many gates built by the ancestors, allowing them to travel back and forth between the Stars. Asag has shown Merci the location of all nine Gates and explained that each gate corresponded to a different realm, and in each realm, there was a God who ruled. There was God the father, The All, God of the Jews, The father of The Christ. Allah who was the god of the Muslims and the teacher of Muhammad, Odin was a Norse god, and Thor was his son. Zeus ruled over Olympus,

Horus was the Egyptian god whose son was Osiris, and Ra, The Egyptian god of the sun.

Additionally, there were teachers like Buddha and Vishnu; each of these Gods held dominion over their own respective realms. This knowledge was overwhelming, yet it opened a world of possibilities for Merci, realizing that her journey was not just about discovering her own identity but also about understanding the intricate web of divine beings that shape the cosmos.

In the celestial chambers of Nibiru, comic tension weighed heavy. Antu's distress over Merci's disappearance had cast a cloud over the entire atmosphere.

"Look, mother," Enki said, his tone measured and calm, "if Merci's life force were ended, you have a connection to her, which is the universal cord that binds you. If it were cut, would you not know it?" Her life force is strong and vibrant, even if it's not as perceptible as before

Antu nodded, though her uncertainty remained. She had always been able to tune into Merci's presence, but now, that connection felt void shrouded in mystery. "The alignment of the stars is significant," Ninhursag interjected, her voice carrying a sense of ancient wisdom,

"This may very well be a sign of her Transcendence. If she were not alive, this cosmic event would not be unfolding." Exchanging a knowing glance within Ninhursag, Enki held on to a truth he did not share; he was privy to more about Merci's current situation. As much as he wanted to alleviate his family's worry, he understood the importance of maintaining the delicate threads of fate.

Suddenly, Ishtar enters the chamber, a whirlwind of energy and determination. After having returned to earth successfully because the king had given her the task of ending Asmodeus's reign of terror, she told her sister that this made way for her to find Merci, relaying the developments that had transpired with Merci's friends and Detective Black.

She also told them of the death of Merci's boyfriend and the incident at her off-campus house. Even though Ishtar exuded power and confidence, beneath it lay a bit of apprehension. "Take care, sister," Ninhursag cautioned, her eyes filled with a mixture of sisterly concern and the wisdom of the ages, "Asmodeus is no ordinary adversary; he senses the currents of fate as much as we do, and he will be prepared for your arrival. Binding him won't be as simple as before."

Acknowledging the gravity of the situation and knowing that this confrontation was not just about her and Asmodeus but about the intricate interplay of destinies that were convening and converging upon the world, Ishtar couldn't help but think about Merci, lost in time, as well as the urgency to find her.

As the cosmic tapestry continued to weave the threads of their fates, Ishtar readied herself for the journey ahead. It wasn't just about facing demons; it was about Merci's well-being, the power that Merci would someday wheel—her understanding of her lineage, and the connection that binds Merci to mankind. Merci held the key to everyone's fate.

Asag taught Merci about a Majestic Assembly that she would one day be a part of called The Council of the Shepherds of the heavens; they reigned Supreme. This celestial governing body held dominion over the multiverse, their decisions echoing through time and the universe like a cosmic ripple.

Each member, a deity, a ruler presiding over their respective kingdoms, which extended far beyond mortal comprehension. Bound by an intricate unity, they formed the council, convening to deliberate upon matters that would shape The Grand Design of the multiverse itself when the concept of humanity was to be realized.

The Anunnaki stood chosen among the cosmic Pantheon. Their mastery of genetics and a profound understanding of DNA positioned them to undertake the monumental task. Bestowed with this divine mandate, they forged the creation of a new race, one fashioned to be stewards of the earth and to fulfill the needs that the Grand universe demanded.

At the outset, these primordial workers could not procreate, although they were crafted with precision. When the council saw the creation for them, this was a fruitful outcome; the Divine Council of the Shepherds of the Heavens found the creation before them to be remarkable.

The cosmos resonated with approval as the first humans walked the nascent Earth, a blend of Divine essence and Earthly matter. As the dawn of this new era unfolded, the members of the council orchestrated the division of the planet. Each deity is Sovereign in their Celestial domain, imparting their distinct wisdom and codes of living to the fledgling human race.

The cosmic patrons became mentors, each contributing to the comprehensive tapestry of knowledge that would guide these beings in navigating the intricacies of their new existence. The Gods dispensed teachings that would eventually coalesce into various cultures and civilizations. The humans, bound to them the ethereal and corporeal, flourished under the diverse influences of the Divine benefits.

These Celestial laws for living were intertwined with every fabric of human society, laying the foundation for diverse systems of belief, ethics, and governance. Yet, even as humans thrived under the guidance of their celestial mentors, whispers of challenges to come began to resume through the corridors of destiny. The council, wise and farsighted, knew that the tapestry they had woven would face many tests of endurance.

Merci was standing at the threshold of a new Journey. The gateway to ancient Earth beckoned to her. Her heart brimmed with gratitude towards Asag for his unwavering support throughout her transformative Journey. Knowing that without his guidance, she might never have made it this far.

As she bid her silent thanks and farewell, she cast one last glance over her shoulder with a mixture of determination and uncertainty in her eyes.

For Asag, watching her depart was an act of faith; even though he was a demon, he had faith and confidence that Merci possessed the strength and resilience to face the challenges ahead. Yet, a nagging worry lingered in the recesses of his mind, knowing that Erra was still in pursuit, continuing his relentless hunt for Merci. So, he decided to shadow her from a distance; he was skilled in masking his presence, ensuring that Merci's heightened senses would not detect him; his silent visual was a testament to his concern for her safety and love.

With each step, Merci and Ishtar's path converged upon their chosen destinations. A sense of shadowing hung in the air. The surroundings were dark with sinister symbols, an ominous testament to the presence of dark forces. As Ishtar and Detective Black emerged from the car, the very street seemed to come alive, every onlooker turning their gaze in her direction as though they recognized her.

A chilling aura of recognition washed over her, signaling that her arrival had not gone unnoticed. With each step, the mystery deepened, and Ishtar knew that confronting

Asmodeus would not be a task that was taken lightly. The forces they were about to face were ancient and formidable, and "the looming conflict would test their fundamental nature."

"What can we do for you?" one of the gathered individuals asked, a hint of sarcasm in their tone. "It looks like you're lost. You don't belong here. I think you should leave while you still can." Just then, Detective Black revealed his badge, prompting laughter from the group. "That holds no power here," a young woman said, stepping forward, her gaze fixed on Ishtar. It was the same woman that the detective and his partner had encountered at the occult store before going to Egypt.

"Hello, Detective," the woman greeted with an air of familiarity, "Funny seeing you here."

But the detective couldn't shake the feeling that her attention was divided, as her focus remained on Ishtar.

"Who's your friend?" she inquired, her eyes remaining fixed on Ishtar. The introductions continued with Ishtar being introduced as Dr. Estelle Lowe; however, the woman's response indicated that she was aware of Ishtar's true identity.

"Oh really? That's what you're calling yourself these days?"

Her gaze remained unyielding, her scrutiny revealing that she knew exactly who Ishtar was. The tension between the two women was evident in the exchange of words and unspoken glances.

"Since you ladies seem to be the experts here, what can you tell me so that I can solve these cases? We still have a lot of missing people from all over the world," Detective Black insisted.

"As I told you before, the gate to hell will soon open, and your kind will perish," the shopkeeper responded ominously.

"Not if I can help it," Ishtar retorted, "and make sure to tell your master it is him I have come for."

With those words, Ishtar turned and walked away. The detective was left speechless and unable to formulate a response. He simply followed her back to the car. Once they were in the car, he couldn't contain his confusion. "What the hell was that all about?" he asked.

Ishtar's reply was cryptic yet revealing, "That is the Keeper of the Flame."

"The keeper of what?" he questioned.

"The Keeper of the flame that guards the gates of hell," Ishtar explained. The detective was baffled. "How do you know that?" "We have met before. She is his contact," Ishtar replied calmly. "Whose contact?" asked Detective Black.

"The demon Asmodeus" was her reply. The detective's memory stirred.

"Do you mean the one who came from the upside-down pyramid?"

Ishtar nodded, "Yes."

"But when I first met her," the detective said, "she was talking about demons that were as old as time itself. That was before the pyramid was open, so it was not your Asmodeus that she was talking about."

"No, it's not; it's the Sebittu and the Hallaku," clarified Ishtar, "The Richardson murder and the one at Merci's off-campus house were not done by Asmodeus."

Detective Black's perplexity deepened, "So the removal of the eyes and organs, what does that imply?" he asked.

Ishtar's gaze remained intense, "it's the way of the Hallaku and the Sebittu; they remove the eyes to see what lies beyond our reality, to gain insight from the other side."

Detective Black's brow furrowed in obvious contemplation, "So these demons are the ones responsible for all the ritualistic murders we've been encountering?"

Ishtar nodded solemnly, "Yes, many of them. These are very ancient, malevolent entities; they have a connection to this city that predates even Asmodeus' recent emergence."

As the car continued on its path through the city, Detective Black couldn't shake off a very unsettling feeling. He had already encountered Asmodeus and was aware of the danger that he posed.

"Who are they searching for?" asked Detective Black, his curiosity changed to unease.

Ishtar's reluctance to reveal everything only fueled his determination to uncover the truth. The goddess hesitated, carefully weighing her response. She didn't want to disclose that they were after Merci. Detective Black might have been challenging to work with, but he wasn't a fool. She didn't want to get caught in a web of explanations. Countering his question with one of her own, "Who do you think they're looking for?" Considering her question, the Detective said, "I'm not entirely certain yet, but I'm convinced it is all tied to your niece."

"Why do you think that?" asked Ishtar, her tone casual but her gaze sharp. Leaning back in the seat and letting out a slow breath, the Detective spoke, "The Richarson murder and your niece's roommate's boyfriends, those two murders are distinct from the others, and they both have a direct connection to your niece; moreover, the timing coincides with the pyramid's discovery in the desert, she was there, and then she vanished. She's the epicenter of all these events."

The tension in the car grew noticeable. Ishtar's silence hinted to the detective that there was more she knew about everything but chose to withhold it, leaving Detective Black with a growing sense that there was far more to this puzzle than met the eye. During the day, Ishtar partnered with Detective Black to unravel the mysteries behind these perplexing cases, but as the sun dipped below the horizon, she shed her Earthly facade, revealing the true Goddess of War beneath.

Under the shroud of night, she combed the city, relentlessly seeking out all forms of malevolence, obliterating any evil that dared to cross her path. Her quest persisted, a relentless pursuit of Asmodeus and Merci. Remaining convinced that it was not the demon Asmodeus that held Merci captive. Then, like a sudden whisper, Ishtar felt it. A flicker of Merci's life force. She harnessed every ounce of her Divine power, homing in on the signal, yet she was not the sole recipient of the sensation. Across the Cosmic Web, Antu, the mother of the Gods, sensed it too.

Asag relayed a message to Enki, informing him of Merci's readiness and her journey to Sumerian. Enki recognizes this as the opportune moment to meet his little sister. Transforming into human form, the god of the air walked the Earthly realm, eager to be the first human contact Merci would make.

Exiting the Stargate, Merci felt an inexplicable presence as if she were not alone. Asag's teachings echoed in her mind, urging her to heed her instincts. Telling her it would always guide her to the truth. Sensing the inexorable pull of the gate, she was yanked forward, landing face first in the dirt of this ancient realm, struggling to rise gracefully. Merci couldn't help but blush in embarrassment.

A few curious onlookers observed her ordeal. While in the corner, a man in the attire of a servant stood, amusement dancing in his eyes as he strolled towards her, his laughter bubbling forth, offering her assistance. "Are you okay?" he asked with genuine concern, extending a helpful hand as he introduced himself, "Hello, I'm Enki." Meeting his gaze, Merci felt a sense of safety; his name sounded familiar, yet she wasn't sure from where, but she accepted his assistance. Knowing that once she touched him, she could read him, still, once his hand touched hers, she felt nothing. She expressed her gratitude before resuming her journey.

Nippur, the cradle of civilization and Merci's birthplace. It unfurled its vibrant tapestry as she traversed its ancient streets. Life pulsed through every street in the city. The aroma of fresh bread filled the air, as well as the laughter of children at play, merchants hawked sacred wares, and the tantalizing scent of smoked meats made her hungry.

The skyline was adorned with magnificent temples, each dedicated to a different deity. Among them was Enlil's temple, a structure she recalled from her past visits. Now complete and towering above the others as the Grand Temple grew near, memories of Prince Liam and his mother and the warmth that they showed her resurfaced.

A decision formed in Merci's mind; she'd pay them a visit. Lost in her thoughts, she unwittingly vocalizes them.

"Go see who?" the kind stranger inquired, drawing Merci's attention. "Oh, no one," Merci responded quickly, masking her true intentions. The bustling surroundings of the Market made conversation difficult, but the stranger's interests intrigued her.

Enki continued guiding her through the Labyrinth streets, acknowledging her question about navigating the city. "Yes, it's quite a challenge to move around here. This Market is the heart of trade and commerce; it's where everything is bought and sold." The heat was intense as the atmosphere buzzed with activity.

Amid the hustle and bustle, Enki shared more insights. "Today is especially busy," Enki stated, "it's one of the Market's peak days. The heart of Nippur's religious and economic life converges here."

The symphony of voices, the vibrant colors of goods, and the scent of various offerings created a sensory masterpiece that enveloped them as they moved forward.

"The strength of Nippur's religious tradition gives the city its longevity," he explained as they navigated the bustling Market. "Most of the land is owned by the temples, and this is where goods are produced and manufactured. The temples hold a significant role within the economy and the government, alongside the private sector," Enki continued to provide insights into the city's dynamics.

"Nippur is quite expansive, and due to its size, it is not safe for a woman to wander alone here," he cautioned.

Merci couldn't help but react to his assumptions, "So you think I need you to protect me?"

"Yes, you do," he acknowledged, "your attire and your speech are distinct from this area. Besides, I know most of the women of Nippur, and this is the first time I've seen you."

Merci's patience began to wear thin. "Look," she said, "I don't want to be rude, but you're really getting on my nerves. If I let you accompany me, you will do it in silence. Agreed?"

"Okay," he relented, realizing that he had pushed too far. Still, his thoughts were not hidden from her. Merci heard his last thought about her eyes resembling those of his mother. Now, the conversations between them took a curious turn. "Enki, I don't know who or what you are, but you are not some lowly servants," she spoke candidly, "My essence doesn't reject you."

Before he could respond, she vanished, leaving Enki startled. He swiftly called out to Asag, seeking answers, but Asag seemed to have disappeared as well.

Ishtar returned to her sister's side with exhilarating news, but she was halted by Antu's intervention. Antu informed her that she had insight into Merci's whereabouts; Asag had been safeguarding Merci, and although her exact location was unknown, the one certainty was that she was alive.

Era had come tantalizingly close to capturing her, but her incredible speed thwarted his grasp, yet he knew that her unique DNA would lead him directly to her. Asag, however, had other intentions.

Asag found Anu, urgently sharing, "My king, I've located the Royal heir, though she is embroiled in a life-and-death battle; unless you intervene, she will be killed." Asag knew that the king wanted her alive.

"Who poses the threat?"

"Erra," Asag replied.

Anu had specified Merci's survival. In response, the king harnessed his Cosmic power, creating a seismic shock that shattered time itself, effectively rendering an end to Erra.

Seizing the moment, Enki swiftly swept Merci away, straight to the Queen's chamber. Merci found herself embraced by Ishtar. "Mother," Merci cried in recognition. Ishtar gently pushed her in Antu's direction. Then she said, "Merci, as I am sure you are aware, I was only the one entrusted to protect you. This is your mother."

Antu couldn't help but smile, remarking, "I see you met your brother." Merci looked at them, then back at Ishtar with a hint of playful pride. Ishtar nudged her again gently towards the queen. Merci met her mother's gaze and then her brother's and, with a smile, said, "That's why I felt I could trust you, Enki."

The king summoned them all to the Great Hall; he wanted answers, and he wanted them now. The fate of Nibiru and The Anunnaki hung in the balance, and he was determined to uncover the truth. He had decided that the time for secrecy was over, and the truth about Merci's lineage must be revealed.

Chapter 15: Royal Heir Identified

Nibiru, the enigmatic Planet of The Crossing, is as ancient as time itself; its culture and atmosphere are woven into the very fabric of its history and civilization. A Celestial body with a highly elliptical orbit, Nibiru's life cycles, traditions, and societal rhythms were intricately shaped by its Celestial dance with its sun and the cosmic vastness beyond.

The skies of Nibiru were a spectacle of mesmerizing color, bathed in rich hues of deep purples, iridescent blues, and fiery oranges. The planet's elliptical orbit brings it both close to its sun and far away, leading to dramatic variations in temperature. An atmospheric composition. During its proximity to the sun, the atmosphere is charged with vibrant energy, causing shimmering auroras to dance across the heavens.

The terrain of Nibiru a blend of all inspiring landscapes, vast crystalline deserts glistened under the sun's radiance, while lust forests teemed with unique flora and fauna that thrive in Nibiru's ever-changing environment. Enigmatic oceans reflect the vivid colors of the skies above, and the towering mountain ranges echo the planet's majestic character.

The inhabitants of Nibiru, the Anunnaki, are a race of profound intellectual powers with spiritual insight. Their cultural identity is intrinsically linked to the cosmic forces that shape their world. They perceive themselves as Cosmic guardians entrusted with preserving the delicate balance between science, spirituality, and nature.

The cities on Nibiru are architectural marvels that seamlessly blend with nature and the natural landscape. These cities serve as hubs of knowledge and innovation, housing sprawling libraries, advanced laboratories, and sacred temples dedicated to The All.

The cosmic Celestial force that influences their lives. The arts flourish on Nibiru, with intricate sculptures capturing the essence of cosmic beauty and vibrant paintings depicting the interplay of light and energy in the universe. Music resonates throughout their cities, harmonizing with the rhythm of celestial bodies and invoking a sense of unity among the Anunnaki.

As the inhabitants of Nibiru explore the far reaches of the cosmos, their insatiable curiosity fuels their technological advancements. Their society reveres both ancient wisdom and cutting-edge knowledge, fostering a holistic understanding of the universe. The prophecy of the royal heir is interwoven with Nibiru's Cosmic tapestry, guided by the pulse of celestial energies. Merci's journey holds the potential to reshape her destiny and that of this planet, as well as to unlock the mysteries of its past and future. The King's summons echoed throughout the palace, drawing every member of the royal family and their trusted advisors to the Great Hall.

Anu's powerful presence sat upon the grand throne, symbolizing his authority over Nibiru. Antu, Ishtar, and Ninhursag entered the hall together, their faces a mix of determination and trepidation. This was the moment they had long anticipated, a moment when secrets would be unveiled. "Your majesties," Anu began, his voice resolute, "We have kept secrets hidden for millennia, but the time has come for them to be known," motioning for Merci to step forward.

Her every step echoed in the hushed hall. Standing before the throne, she felt the weight of her destiny pressing upon her. "Our Royal heir," the king proclaimed, his voice ringing with authority, "She, who was born in a distant past and protected throughout the ages." Merci bowed her head, respectfully acknowledging her role in this celestial drama. The king's attention turned to the Queen and her sisters, who were in tears, "Speak the truth, my beloveds," he urged gently. The King's imposing presence filled the Great Hall.

His eyes, like orbs of authority, scan the room, demanding answers, wanting to know the extent of the queen and her sister's involvement. The time for secrecy was over; the truth would be revealed, or consequences would follow.

Antu, Ishtar, and Ninhursag stood before their king expressionless. It was a pivotal moment; the destiny of the royal heir and the fate of Nibiru teetered on the balance. Tensions in the Great Hall reached the zenith as the queen revealed her truth.

In the echoes of the Great Hall, the Queen stood before her husband, Anu, the ruler of Nibiru; her voice resonated with a mixture of regret and determination as she addressed the assembly of her peers. "May I address you, my king, before this esteemed House?" she asked, her eyes fixed on Anu. The king responded with a nod. With a deep breath, she continued, "I am the mother of this child. It is I who brought her to this life."

The Great Hall trembled with the weight of Antu's revelation. Her confession hung in the air: a truth that could unravel the tapestry of secrets woven around Merci's existence. The king, once brimming with fury, was now perplexed; his Queen had concealed the truth, a truth that could change the course of their kingdom's destiny.

Addressing her, his voice, a mixture of astonishment and inquiry, "You led me to believe that she was merely an anomaly, a blend of our DNA within the human host." The king added, "Why keep this hidden, Antu?"

Her Regal continence, softened by the sorrow of her concealed secret, replied with a heavy heart, "I did it out of fear, my love. Fear for her life and mine. I didn't want you to know the full extent of her origin."

Anu's eyes boar into hers, seeking answers. "Her father, who is he?"

Antu hesitated, knowing the revelation of Merci's true parentage could have far-reaching consequences. She finally replied, "She is born of our love; I merely infused her genome with a trace of human DNA."

Anu, struggling to comprehend the intricate web of deception, demanded, "But how is that even possible?" Enki, sensing the tension and recognizing the fragile balance, steps forward. "Father, I, too, was unaware of the entire truth. I only knew that mother had been gravely ill during her pregnancy. She took on human form to shield the fetus. The child was delivered as human, and fearing your anger, she left her in the care of the humans."

The room was awash with heavy silence, for the truth has always been a complex entity and tangled with the fate of Nibiru as well as the safeguarding of the royal heir. "So, this is why you hid her from me? Because she was born human?" Anu stated, his voice tingling with a mixture of realization and concern, and the queen nodded solemnly, "Yes, my love, it was because of her humanity that I wanted her to have the chance to walk amongst those you love."

Anu remained skeptical of his Queen's explanation; he had sired children with humans before, but this child, with her unique blend of human and divine DNA, carried the mark of royalty. Before the tension could escalate further, another presence entered the Great Hall; it was Enlil.

His arrival was marked by haste and anger, and he was upset that he had not been the one to find the Royal heir. "Welcome," Enlil said, his voice dripping with disdain. "Welcome to the kingdom of the creators of all mankind, including you. I am Enlil," the atmosphere grew sinister.

Antu rose to stop the hostility as it became evident. However, Anu swiftly interrupted his words firmly,

"Enough, "he said, "Is this how you greet the royal heir? The prophecy foretold that she would someday rule this Kingdom, and we must treat her accordingly."

Enlil's mind filled with resentment. He promised to do everything in his power to ensure that Merci would never ascend to the throne. Anu now turned his gaze to Merci and inquired, "By what name shall we address you?"

Merci glanced briefly at Ishtar for guidance and replied with a respectful tone, "Your Majesty, sir, my name is Merci."

A warm smile crossed Anu's face, "fitting," he said as he extended his welcome. "Young lady, you can call me father," he said, embracing her with open arms. Merci felt a sense of belonging and acceptance as she was welcomed into the Royal House of Anunnaki. Anu then dismissed the room, leaving only Enki in his presence. Antu, Merci's mother, took her to her new chamber within the Royal house, where she was introduced to her siblings. Some of them harbored mixed feelings about her existence, but her aunts tried their best to make her feel at home.

Stepping into her chamber, she couldn't help but feel a sense of awe. It was a strange but beautiful place like nothing she'd ever known. With the Grandeur and Mystique that now surrounded her, Merci couldn't help but wonder what the destiny that awaited her in this new world was. Merci's first visit to Nibiru was a journey of wonder and amazement as she stepped onto the soil of a world that felt both ancient and futuristic.

The moment her feet touched the ground, she could sense the pulsating energy of the planet resonating through every fiber of her being. The sky above her was a breathtaking canvas of colored hues that on Earth she had never witnessed, deep purple's merge with iridescent Blues, casting a surreal glow over the landscape.

A distant sun radiated warmth, yet there was a celestial coolness in the air that made her senses tingle with anticipation. Before her sprawled a magnificent city, its architecture blended seamlessly with the land's natural beauty.

Towers of iridescent crystals seem to rise from the very planet, reflecting the colors of the sky in a dazzling display. The city's layout was unlike anything she'd ever seen on Earth: organic, harmonious, and meticulously designed to honor both the land and the cosmos. As Merci walked through the city streets, she was met with welcoming smiles from the Anunnaki inhabitants. They were people of striking beauty, their features radiant and their eyes gleaming with knowledge.

Each person seems to emit an aura of reverence for the celestial forces that shape their lives. The air was filled with a soft melody of ethereal music, a harmonious composition that resonated with the rhythm of the universe. Merci found herself drawn to a magnificent temple, a sacred Sanctuary dedicated to the cosmic forces that the Anunnaki revered, The All. Upon entering, she was enveloped by an atmosphere of serenity and spiritual resonance.

Inside, she encountered beings engaged in deep meditation and rituals, their movements synchronized with the celestial rhythms. The temple's walls were adorned with intricate murals depicting the cosmic dance of planets and stars, a visual representation of the connection between Nibiru and the universe beyond.

A grand feast in Merci's honor was announced, and Anu planned to introduce her to all the inhabitants of the Universe from the different kingdoms scattered across the galaxies. The prospect of this overwhelming event left Merci feeling exhausted. All she truly desired was some rest; the luxurious bed in her chamber appeared exceptionally inviting, and without hesitation, she dropped her bag and fell onto it.

In her semi-conscious state, Merci overheard her mother and aunts discussing their intentions to reimprison Asmodeus, the demon who was causing so much turmoil.

Time seemed to rush forward relentlessly, and Merci found herself immersed in an intensive education about her royal lineage.

She was trained in the ways of a warrior princess with Ishtar herself as her instructor; after all, who could better teach the art of warfare than the goddess of war herself? Although some knowledge seemed to come to Merci instinctively, she diligently honed her skills alongside her physical training. Merci dug deep into the ancient archives, expanding her understanding of Enochian Magic, an ancient and potent form of magic.

As she learned, Merci came to comprehend that her true power would only manifest once her Transcendence was complete. She also accessed the story of the creation of humankind, as told in the Sumerian creation story. Merci sighed and remarked to her mother, learning about all the different alien races that inhabited within the expansive universe feels like my brain is about to burst.

Antu, understanding the weight of Merci's studies, replied, "I know, my dear, but you must strive to understand each one of them. It's essential to your role."

The moment had finally arrived for The Ball in her honor, but Merci's legs felt like they were encased in boulders of ice, making each step a monumental effort. Her mind was racing ahead eagerly, but her body seemed reluctant as if it were held back by an invisible bond. Her anxiety was compounded by the unexpected realization there were no mirrors anywhere in sight. All her time in Nibiru, she had noticed the absence of mirrors. Vanity, perhaps, but the absence of a reflection was disconcerting.

She was longing to see how she looked. Even the most magnificent attire meant little if one couldn't appreciate one's own appearance. All the servants departed, leaving Merci in solitude; the silence in the chamber became profound. Questions swirled in her mind. *Where was her mother? Her sister's? Had they all forgotten?* A wave of loneliness swept over her, but then she took the first step.

As she entered the Grand Hall, Merci's apprehension transformed into awe; she was radiant, a true goddess in every sense of the word. All her previous doubts about her looks vanished. On this day, she, the one they all bowed before her. She appeared before the court in full Glory.

The entire assembly bowed their heads in reverence as she walked in. Her hair cascaded softly against her caramel skin, perfectly complemented by the Exquisite white gown that seemed to caress every curve, reluctant to let go. The jewels dawning the Golden Crown she wore sparkled and danced in the light, accentuating the blue of her eyes.

Amid her nervousness, she glanced at the assembled crowd. On her left, she spotted the Agrarians, offering a gracious nod in their direction accompanied by a warm smile. The Agrarian's presence is immediately recognizable as Asiatic Nordic humans.

To her right were the Afim, hailing from the constellation Lyra; they were small in stature with distinctive spotty skin. Next to them were the Arcticians, known as the Brotherhood of the Galactic Command.

The Protectors of the universe. Their formidable Starship, The Athena, was a symbol of their dominance and dedication to safeguarding the cosmos.

Further along the assembly, Merci's gaze fell upon the Alpha Draconian. These reptilian beings harbored intentions of invading Earth, fueled by the belief that advanced technology should be kept from the masses. They feared that humans, with their potential for interplanetary and interstellar expansion, posed a future threat.

In contrast, the Alpha Centaurians, known as the scientists of the galaxy, held the view that mankind should be given the knowledge of advanced technology, and in an attempt to share their wisdom, they crash-landed a starship filled with advanced technology in Roswell, New Mexico.

These beings existed on a higher plane of knowledge. Among the attendees were the Akim, often referred to as the elder race of the Nephilim, as mentioned in biblical texts. Along with them were the Antarcticians representing a Subterranean Human Society… The Ashtar Command was also present, comprising a fleet of extraterrestrial aircraft responsible for protecting the solar system. With a force of 20 million, they were a formidable presence. Commander Ashtar led this vast fleet, offering their services to the Royal Heir, emphasizing their connection to the Angelic Kingdom.

The grand assembly included every member of the Andromeda Council, a vital component of the Galactic Federation. Their directive was clear: all alien races with a presence on Earth and the Moon were ordered to leave the planets immediately. The council's intent was to observe how Humanity would interact and thrive without external manipulation, a status quo that had persisted for the past 5,723 years.

Merci glanced around, quietly confident in her knowledge. This she thought would be a straightforward task, having learned about every race. She now knew that the Alpha Draconian were formidable figures; they were feared throughout the Universe for their previous attempt to reclaim the earth, driven by apprehensions about human overpopulation, pollution, and environmental challenges.

These creatures understood humanity and its inherited Warrior instincts and their ceaseless drive for progress. Fearing that Earth's inhabitants might turn their sites towards the cosmos. The Draco's believed that allowing humans to take over the universe with limited knowledge would lead to its destruction. The Alcobata, on the other hand, sent an envoy to greet Merci, even though they were not officially invited. They hailed from the constellation Perseus, and they were an aggressive race, commanding numerous ships and colonizing hundreds of planets. These parasitic beings had minimal interaction with other alien races and were known for frequent visits to the earth, often linked to human abductions.

As Merci considered this diverse assembly of cosmic entities, she understood the complexities that lay ahead in her role as the Royal heir. Merci's head began to spin, and just as she was on the brink of fainting, Asag swept her away. They twirled and laughed like in the days when she was solely his royal one, but now she was destined to be Queen for an entire Kingdom.

However, at that moment, it was just the two of them, and no one else existed. Just as Asag leaned in to kiss Merci, her sisters, Ninlil and Ninki, called out to her with great news to deliver. "Sister, we have wonderful news," they said. Merci inquired what it was. Ninlil replied, "There is talk of a royal union."

"A royal union?" Merci asked, puzzled.

Her older sister, Ninlil, replied, "Yes, a royal marriage with another royal family." Perplexed, Merci questioned, "So, who's getting married?" Nikki answered with a smile, "You!" Merci's face revealed her surprise. "I'm not marrying anyone," she protested. "Adonis was the only man I will ever love, and he's not here, so there will be no husband for me."

Deep in thought, Merci considered her feelings. Asag suddenly came to mind, and she realized she had developed feelings for him. However, she also knew that the Asag she had spent time with was not his true form. Thinking out loud, she mused, "He's invisible, and he smells like death." Her sisters erupted in laughter, although they were already aware of who she was referring to.

First in line was the son of the Attamuluk King; their ancient civilization had faced defeat in ancient India against the reptoids, compelling them to leave Earth despite their advanced technology. Merci was not particularly interested, yet she maintained a respectful demeanor as her father directed him onward.

Next came the son of the Aiannan king, hailing from a Martian race in the constellation Gemini. For millennia, they had maintained bases on Mars and mined gold-like minerals there. They were the first to visit Earth in 1235 BC, in Japan. Following closely was the prince from the Airelle Kingdom, who originated from the constellation Ophiuchus. They were a peaceful, nocturnal race who only used Earth as a brief stop on their journeys throughout the multiverse.

The Son of the Alabram king continued to speak to Merci telepathically, revealing that he hailed from a planet beyond the Andromeda Galaxy, explaining that although they resembled humans in appearance, Earth beings could never survive on his planet due to the weak oxygen levels. Describing his home planet as home to millions, like earth, but with unique abilities. Their large brains allowed them to absorb information through Osmosis.

Next, the Bootian Prince approached with a lavish assortment of gifts, including silks, satins, and exquisite fabrics. He introduced the Bootans, who were part of the Salamani Confederation from the constellation Boots, situated 40 light years from earth. Candidly disclosing their malevolent intentions towards humans, viewing them as a potential food source. The Bootans were aligned with the Orion group and held hostile beliefs towards humans, considering them inferior.

Merci was quick to dismiss any thought of marriage with them, as she suspected she might end up as dinner on her wedding night. Then, she encountered the widowed King of the Blues, a being with transparent blue skin, large almond eyes, and a notably short stature. Sharing with Merci their belief in pursuing one's passion and following one's true path, they adhered to the doctrine of do and be what you are.

While she could tolerate such a lifestyle, she couldn't fathom the possibility of having blue-skinned children, so she dismissed the idea.

In 1947, the United States government received communication from the Grays, but the Blues warned against making any deals with them, foreseeing disaster for Humanity and the planet; instead, the Blues advocated for teaching peace and harmony.

Since mankind refused to disarm and listen, the military declared disinterest in peace and harmony, prompting the Blues to depart from the planet; however, a few Blues chose to remain and entered into a treaty with the Hopi Indians, who affectionately called them the blue star Warriors.

Merci felt like the introductions had been endless, and after a while, she stopped paying attention to what was being said. Antu could see her growing overwhelmed, so she approached the king and whispered in his ear, "Darling, don't you think this is enough for the day? We can continue the introductions tomorrow if that's alright with you."

Observing Merci's exhaustion, the king understood and realized that her human mind needed rest. He graciously asked his guests to excuse the royal heir and announce that the introductions would resume the following day, and with that, he dismissed the assembly.

Merci was elated to hear the guests being excused; she exchanged pleasantries and hurried to her chamber, hoping to find some peace where Enlil awaited her.

Startling her at first, but upon recognizing him, she inquired, "What do you want, Enlil?"

"I just wanted some time with you," he replied, "You've been so busy since you arrived, and we haven't really had a chance to get to know each other."

Merci, feeling tired, retorted, "So you want us to get to know each other? What do you really want, Enlil? Because right now, I'm tired." Enlil appeared to accept her need for rest. "We can talk later," he said as he left the room. Merci was relieved, convinced that he had ulterior motives, but for now, all she wanted was some rest.

The days seemed to go as usual, filled with lessons upon lessons. Merci couldn't help but notice that Ishtar had been absent more frequently lately. She started to wonder where her aunt disappeared to during these times. *Maybe she had a lover somewhere.* Merci thought to herself, letting her imagination Wander.

Curious, she attempted to locate Ishtar, using her telepathic abilities; however, Ishtar had already taken precautions to block Merci's powers, ensuring they wouldn't affect anyone in the Royal family, preventing her from tracking her aunt.

The kingdom was all a buzz with energy, and Merci's presence seemed to elevate everyone around her. Finally, having found the family she had always longed for, and the kingdom adored her. As she prepared for her war strategy lessons, Merci eagerly anticipated seeing Ishtar again.

"Time to get to work," Merci declared as she welcomed the goddess of war. Before they could dive into the lessons, Merci couldn't help but ask, "Aunty, where do you go when you're away from the kingdom?"

Ishtar replied, "Well, Merci, I am the goddess of war; my work never ends. There will always be wars and rumors of wars. Why do you ask?"

Merci hesitated for a moment before responding, "I thought maybe you were still searching for that demon released from the inverted pyramid." Merci voiced her suspicion.

Ishtar knew instantly she wouldn't be able to keep it from her for long, especially since all the elders were discussing it, and the time had come to respond. "Because I hear of the carnage he's causing throughout the Universe," pressing on, Merci continued, "What is it that he looks for?" she asked.

"The keys!"

Merci pressed on, "Which keys? Do you mean the keys that Jesus took when He descended into hell?"

Ishtar nodded gravely, "Yes, and I must stop him."

"May I help you? After all, it is partially my fault he was released," Merci said sincerely.

Ishtar's response was swift and decisive. "You are not ready," she said, her voice filled with authority. With a sudden, powerful gesture, she knocked Merci off her feet. "See, you're not ready," she stated firmly as she left the room. Ishtar knew this would not be the last she would hear from Merci about this subject; after all, she had been her mother for all her life.

Before Merci knew it, it was time for more introductions as her parents searched for a suitable husband. It was just more of the same nonsense. Merci let out a sigh once she saw the endless line of possible suitors; the thought gave her a headache. Noticing today's line was longer than yesterday's, she took a deep breath and took her seat.

Then this one emerged, as if from the pages of The Gods and Men trilogy, tall, tan, and handsome. He was the ruler of the Cetians-Tau-Cetian, and he presented his older son, the Cetians Prince Koli; they hailed from humans, originating from the Mediterranean and South American Seas. Representing a significant conversion of extraterrestrial and human influences closely allied with the Pleiadeans.

As the Cetians departed, the hall grew dark. With the entry of the Butta's, these beings dwelled in spiritual darkness, associated with the haunting tales of children abductions in the night, earning them the ominous title of night dwellers. They radiated negative and aggressive energy, Merci was relieved when they departed the gathering.

Next, she encountered a gentile face belonging to the elder brother of the Chiron's' King; he stood slightly taller than most humans, but his delicate build was a striking feature. Upon closer inspection, Merci noticed he was a hexapod, possessing four legs and two arms. He began recounting Tales of his own world. The Chir Garden Paradise explains that over a thousand years ago, his species almost obliterated themselves in a nuclear war, seeing many parallels with the human race's potential path.

Then came the chameleons, a race of reptilians genetically engineered to assume a human appearance using technosis and molecular shape-shifting; they employed Holograms to maintain a convincing human facade, and rumor circulated about their joint operational facilities near Dolce and various other locations throughout the planet.

These individuals were not ordinary guests; they were mercenaries, part of an advanced scouting party with ominous plans for a silent invasion to seize control of human society. Among them were the Dero's, a perilous species known to dwell underground; they were believed to have once been human and now transformed into the stuff of Legends, trolls, and leprechauns, demented cave dwellers with ambitions of taking over Earth.

Their intellect was limited, and trust in them was ill-advised.

Merci observed the crowd before her parting, creating a path as if guided by an unseen force. It wasn't Moses who approached her, but rather the king of the Draco's, the most dreaded among the reptoid species; his name, Draco the First, was also the name of the astronomical constellation that houses the Draconian empire. In a proposition that was nothing short of audacious, Draco offered Merci his entire empire in exchange for her becoming his 900th wife. However, she respectively declined.

The Draco's constituted a highly advanced society with an inherently hostile and perilous disposition. They held the belief that the human species was inherently inferior, asserting their rights to Earth as an outpost from ancient times. Although their home planet could no longer sustain life, they remained. The Great Hall was filled with an illuminous assembly of beings. Among them were The Eight Immortals, each of whom endowed upon Merci a unique gift, the essence and purpose known only to her. They urged her to use these gifts wisely, though the specific reasons remained a mystery, leaving Merci intrigued.

The Ascended Masters were also in attendance. These were her teachers. Amidst this Gathering, the radiant Glory of Yahweh, shown as the Archangel Gabriel, made his entrance, the celestial glow of Heaven surrounded him as he presented Merci with Yahweh's Grace, a Divine gift of immeasurable significance.

Allah himself imparted to Merci the hidden knowledge of the Holy Quran, an act of profound importance.

The Buddha, despite Merci's already being an enlightened physical being, graced her with wisdom beyond human comprehension; however, there was a growing concern among those in attendance. They worried that Merci's human brain, occupying a mere 20% of its full capacity, might soon reach its limit as it struggled to contain the vast knowledge being poured into it.

Anu, the king, sought counsel from the queen in hushed tones; he expressed his concern and asked whether Merci understood the significance necessary for her Transcendence. With a pained look in her eyes, The Queen shook her head and confessed that Merci remained unaware. The completion of her transcendence required her to depart from a human body, a revelation Merci was not yet aware of.

The God Ra sent his son to welcome the Royal heir. He told her that his father wanted her to know that she would always be covered in the warm rays of the Sun, and as he said that, she began to shine as bright as the sun. The whole room was engulfed in light; this power frightened her. She started screaming, "Someone turn it off, please." Ishtar told her to calm down and concentrate because she needed to learn to control these new powers because they could be very destructive if not handled correctly.

Merci's humanity was slowly disappearing. Antu had found it impossible to disclose to Merci the daunting truth that her transcendence required her to part from her human existence. After all of the formal introductions and meeting with eligible suitors, Merci was finally allowed to mingle with her remaining guests. The knowledge of her royal responsibilities had begun to weigh on her, and she couldn't help but express her exhaustion to her mother.

Amid this Grand Gathering, Queen Antu introduced Merci to an array of divine beings. She engaged in a long and intriguing conversation with the god Vishnu. Next, she had the privilege of meeting the God of thunder, Thor, and his father, Oden.

However, her mother's whispered warnings resonated in her ear as she was introduced to Zeus, a deity whose reputation for desire preceded him. Zeus, unabashedly smitten by Merci's human scent and pure innocence, resolved to make her his own. Determined, Zeus was accustomed to attaining whatever he desired, and at time,s it was her. Everyone had extended a warm welcome to the Royal heir.

As time passed, Antu could see that Merci's human body was weakening; she couldn't ignore the visible toll it was taking on her daughter. Her fragile form was slowly deteriorating under the weight of the immense wisdom, knowledge, and power she was absorbing. It was clear to her mother that Merci's physical vessel couldn't withstand this relentless onslaught, and the thought of her enduring such a painful death was unbearable.

Antu, consumed by worry for her daughter, decided to approach the king with her great concern; he, too, was deeply touched by the situation. He cherished all his children equally, yet Merci held a unique and irreplaceable place in his heart due to her extraordinary nature.

The dilemma was that Merci had to undergo a transformation, transcending her human limitations. However, neither the king nor the queen could carry out the necessary action. It was then that Asag, a trusted figure who had played a crucial role in Merci's journey, knocked on the door and entered the king's chamber. The solution presented itself in the form of someone Merci trusted implicitly. Asag willingly offered to be the instrument of

Merci's transcendence, agreeing to assist her in this critical transformation. His only request in return was her hand in marriage.

Asag ardently desired Merci as his wife, even though he was not directly from the Royal lineage of the Sebbitu and the Hallaku; he hoped that the king would find him worthy of such an honor.

Antu knew that Asag had been Merci's steadfast guardian, keeping her from harm while illuminating her path as an Anunnaki heir. For this unwavering dedication, Asag had earned The Queen's eternal gratitude; however, she understood that the decision to choose a life partner would rest on Merci herself.

She begged the king to respect their daughter's autonomy and not compel her into any marriage. He agreed wholeheartedly not to force Merci into any union, but the question remained: would she willingly choose Asag as her eternal companion?

Years had passed since Merci's departure from Earth. She longed to revisit her home planet and see her friends. With a starship gifted by the Andromeda council, Merci asked her elder brother, Enki, to accompany her on this journey. Enki laughed, and this puzzled her, inquiring about his amusement. He gently led her to a seat, taking her hand into his. Amidst his laughter, he shared the harsh truth: her friends on Earth were no more.

Merci's eyes welled with tears as she pressed for details. Enki explained that some had to succumb to old age, while others had met untimely ends due to the ongoing chaos on the planet. Shocked, Merci queried how this could be, given that all her friends were all roughly her age. Enki unraveled the cosmic discrepancy time on Nibiru passed differently from Earth. A single day here equated to a full Earth year; it dawned on Merci that she had spent decades away from our home planet.

The Revelation was not just a temporal shock, but it was a profound emotional upheaval. Her brother continued, "Mother and father have strict rules regarding time travel, particularly how far back or forward you can go," at least until her transcendence was complete.

Her siblings, especially Enki, had emphasized the importance of caution. He warned her that if she were to meet her demise on Earth before her transcendence, her death would be final. Anxious to understand more, Merci asked her brother about when her transcendence would be complete. Enki's response was cryptic, merely assuring her

that it would happen soon. This evasive answer left Merci
even more curious.

Determined to find answers, she headed to her mother's
chamber. It was time to confront the mysterious topic of her
transcendence that everyone seemed to be avoiding. She
couldn't understand why it was such a hushed subject. At
her mother's chamber, Merci overheard her and her aunt
engaged in an intense conversation, discussing matters like
physical and celestial bodies.

Frustrated with the secrecy, Merci decided to enter the
room and confront them directly. Upon entering, she found
not only her mother and aunts but also her father and
brother. What puzzled her even more was the presence of
Asag.

When Merci entered the room, the atmosphere was heavy
with unspoken sorrow, and when they noticed her, everyone
fell into a sudden eerie silence. Their faces were etched
with sadness, their expressions haunted. Merci felt an
unsettled tension in the room; her heart raced as she
questioned why everyone appeared so gloomy. It was as if
a shroud of secrecy and foreboding had descended upon
them.

Ishtar, her aunt, began to move in her direction as if to offer comfort, but she halted, leaving Merci to wonder what could be so profoundly troubling that they couldn't bring themselves to speak of it.

Antu beckoned for Merci to join her, and the solemn expressions on her family's faces sent shivers down her spine. She followed her mother into the chamber, anxiety gnawing at her excitement. "Merci, my child," The Queen began, her voice heavy with concern, "The time is approaching for your transcendence to be completed." Merci's eyes widened with curiosity and a touch of apprehension, "I was wondering when you guys would say something about that. What is transcendence, mother?"

Antu sighed, searching for the right words, "To transcend means to experience life beyond the physical existence that your body has carried. Your soul, which makes you human, shares this body with your celestial essence, a form of pure energy."

Merci, now trying to grasp the concept, "So I have a human body and this Celestial energy?"

"Exactly," said Antu, "we are celestial beings. This is not our true form; we are energy beings. We took on human form because we wanted you to be comfortable. However, the human body is not equipped to handle the immense power and knowledge that you now possess."

Merci frowned, sensing a weighty revelation approaching. "So," she asked, "What does this have to do with me transcending?"

Enki stepped forward, his eyes filled with empathy, "It means you have to leave your physical body."

Merci's heart raced, "Leave my body? How am I supposed to do that?" Asag, who had been quietly listening, spoke, "You have to die, royal one."

Merci's voice trembled with disbelief, "What? What do you mean I have to die?"

Antu nodded as if a profound sadness suddenly engulfed her. As she reached for her daughter, she continued, "You must experience a physical death. Your human mind and body cannot contain the incredible power and knowledge that is now within you; eventually, your body will self-destruct. The human form was never designed for such immense power."

Merci's entire world seemed to spin as the weight of her impending destiny settled upon her; she was to face death, and this she couldn't fully comprehend. All in the name of transcendence. The thought of dying sent shivers down her spine. How could her human mind fully grasp the implications of what they were telling her? Merci was speechless; fear gripped her heart, but she didn't want to show it. With a determined expression, she looked at her family and said, "Don't worry about it, just give me some time to think," as she turned and left the room, needing space to process the weighty information she had just received.

Enki, despite his reassurances, was concerned for his young demi-god sister. He had grown fond of her and felt a responsibility to keep her safe until her transcendence. He knew Merci well enough to understand that he needed to keep an eye on her and prevent her from doing anything human. Deciding to follow her, calling out as he did. "Hey, wait!" Meanwhile, Ishtar was on a mission to locate Asmodeus and retrieve the key he searched for. She knew that finding him wouldn't be easy; he had a reputation for being extremely tricky. Asmodeus had even outsmarted the wisest Man on Earth. The great King Solomon, during the construction of Solomon's temple. Knowing the stakes, Ishtar was determined to find the keys that Jesus had taken during His descent into hell. Ishtar's journey would take her to the kingdom of The Great I Am, where she hoped to uncover the secret of the key.

Asmodeus had been the chief laborer during the construction of Solomon's Temple, albeit not of his own free will. Asmodeus had been controlled by the ring bestowed upon Solomon by God, granting Solomon command over all demons. Asmodeus, having a burning desire to obtain the ring to break free from its control, managed to trick Solomon into surrendering it through cunning manipulation. With the ring in his possession, Asmodeus ascended to King Solomon's throne.

Years later, after wandering the Earth in exile, Solomon managed to regain his throne, gifted with another ring of power. In retribution, he commanded that Asmodeus construct an inverted pyramid. King Solomon helped the goddess of war imprison him. A punishment for his treachery and a safeguard for humanity. For centuries, Asmodeus remained incarcerated within that pyramid, a dormant threat until now.

Having already consulted with the King, Ishtar embarked on a journey to the kingdom of the Alpha and the Omega, seeking the keys, knowing that if she did not destroy these keys, Asmodeus would unleash hell on the Earth. Upon her arrival, she was greeted at the gate by the Archangel Gabriel. Words scarcely describe the beauty of Heaven itself.

The streets were not metaphorically paved with gold; they were quite literally made of precious metal. Ishtar explained the purpose of her visit, and she was guided to a resplendent chamber with a celestial ceiling adorned by Angels, a testament to the unparalleled beauty of Heaven.

This room was an awe-inspiring sight. The Angels were countless, and they sang hymns that filled the air with celestial music. Ishtar marvels at the beauty, realizing that this is the heaven humans all have long to see. A slender Man with a flowing white beard entered the room. "Hello," he greeted, "I am Peter; follow me, please." He escorted Ishtar to the throne room, where she found Yeshua seated at the right hand of his father, radiating divine grace.

"Welcome to our Kingdom. How can we help you?" he asked with a compassionate gaze. Ishtar, with deep regret, replied, "Thank you for allowing my visit. Heavenly Father, I am here in need of the keys to the Gate of Hell. The demon Asmodeus is in search of them, aiming to open the gate and unleash his Legions upon the Earth."

Yahweh nodded solemnly, "We are aware of the Carnage and the butchery he has caused all over the universe. What I would like to know is how he was released. Did you not bind him many millennia ago?"

"Yes, he was released by some archaeologist. Now, he seeks the keys to free all of Hell's evil."

"Our understanding is that your niece had something to do with his release."

"Not exactly," replied Ishtar, "she was attending the Earth School and attempted to stop them from disturbing the Seal of Solomon. However, she was not present at the time of his release."

Yahweh interjected, "Well, the keys will never be found. For I hid them before I ascended to my father."

Ishtar was taken aback by this. "You hid them on Earth?" she asked in total astonishment. Pressing further, her concern was now growing, "but what happens if he finds them? What then? It would be almost impossible to stop the terror."

"We will do what is best for mankind," He replied cryptically. Ishtar could sense the urgency of the situation because Asmodeus grew stronger. The threat he posed to humanity loomed larger than ever. If he were to ever get his hands on the keys, it would unleash terror worse than Pandora's Box.

Peter escorted Ishtar back to the Gates of Heaven and bid her farewell. As Ishtar approached the magnificent gate, she noticed something she hadn't before: how they glowed with an eternal radiance. They were made of pure gold illuminated by an otherworldly light, giving them a pearly white Celestial glow.

Their beauty was beyond description. Suddenly, Ishtar felt Merci's presence calling out her name, "Merci, where are you? I know you're here. Show yourself," she demanded. Merci materialized before her. "What are you doing here, young lady?" Ishtar scolded her, "You know better, Merci."

"Actually, I don't," responded Merci.

"You could have gotten hurt," said Ishtar.

Merci laughed, shrugging nonchalantly, "Come on, auntie, who gets hurt in heaven?"

"That's not the point," Ishtar argued, "You cannot sustain any injury because you can still die."

Merci returned to, "What difference does it make? I got to die anyway. Why not get it over with?"

Knowing the gravity of this situation, Ishtar understood she had to be cautious in her explanation.

"The difference is that when you transcend, it will be under control circumstances," she replied, still using caution. She knew that Asmodeus was on the move, and the fate of not only Merci but all of humanity hung in the balance. Merci was disappointed that Ishtar was upset with her. She just wanted to make her proud, not really comprehending that pride was not one of The Goddess of war's attributes; Arrogance was.

"What's the sense of having all this power if I can't use it?" she asked. "Again, you asked this question, to which we have given you the answers already. Merci," Ishtar replied, "Sternly, you must first transcend. Once you leave that human body and are in your celestial body, then you can do what you will anywhere in the universe. You can do whatever you please, but until then, you will have to obey the rules. Is that clear, young lady?"

"Yes, ma'am," replied Merci reluctantly. She was tired of the limitations and wanted to be free of them. The idea of dying and being reborn scared her, but she was also tired of being treated as if she would break. *"I grew up in Harlem, where you gotta be tough to survive,"* she murmured to herself. Merci knew Ishtar was right. Still, she was tired of restrictions and longed to explore her powers. *"I have all these powers; I liked to explore them,"* she thought out loud. *"Always having been a free spirit, I feel like maybe it's time to get this over with."*

Upon her return home, Merci headed straight for her mother's chamber, calling out, "Are you here, mother?"

"Yes, dear," said the queen.

"Mother, I'm ready to transcend," Merci declared, "so what happens now?"

Antu considered her daughter's words carefully, "Have you considered Asag's offer of marriage?"

"Yes, I have!"

Antu inquired further, "What have you decided?"

"I'll accept his offer," Merci replied thoughtfully, "if he keeps the current body he currently occupies. I've gotten used to it." Besides his true form, Merci's voice tailed off as she contemplated the complexities of her feelings. Her mother loved her, all the while understanding that her daughter was going through something, and she had to let her go through it. The human in Merci didn't understand everything that was materializing in her life.

Ancient languages were not an issue for Merci, so she dug deep into the akashic records, learning about the intricacies of the Hallaku and Sebittu, their history, customs, and their place in the universe. As the days passed, preparation for her wedding continued in the kingdom. The excitement in the air was exhilarating; Merci couldn't help but be consumed by nostalgia. Her thoughts often wandered back to her youth, and the days she and Adonis were young and in love.

Merci had so many questions about her future, about her role as queen, and about the responsibilities that lay ahead. The weight of her impending responsibilities, her impending marriage, and the prospect of Eternity with Asag moved over her. Yet, as she dove into the ancient texts and explored the mysteries of the universe, she couldn't help but feel a glimmer of hope and curiosity about the adventures that awaited her beyond the boundaries of her human existence. Merci's relentless quest for knowledge led her down a path filled with both fascination and trepidation. The information she gathered about her impending transcendence and its incredible power and capabilities surpass human understanding.

However, the more she uncovered, the more ominous the process seemed. The enigmatic expressions she encountered from those who knew about transcendence had left her with a sense of unease. It was clear that this transformation was not going to be a mere walk in the cosmic park. Her physical body, the vessel she had known all her life, had to perish for her to ascend to a higher state of being. What troubled her were the details, the mysterious mechanics of this transformation.

Gleaned those transcended beings possessed extraordinary abilities: telekinesis, aster kinesis, reality manipulation, and even the power to shapeshift. These were not just superhuman attributes; they were godlike. The prospect of such immense power thrilled her as well as terrified her by an equal measure. Yet, the how of it all managed to remain shrouded in ambiguous ambiguity known only to those who had transcended before her.

As Merci moved deeper into her quest, a dark undercurrent of uncertainty flows through her. The cosmos held secrets that begged to be unraveled, but with each revelation came a mounting sense of treacherous transformation, a transformation that would forever alter the essence of who she was.

 Alone in her chamber, lost in the labyrinth of her thoughts about her impending transcendence, Merci was oblivious to her mother's arrival. Queen Antu entered her daughter's chamber with a gentle concern in her eyes, recognizing the turmoil that had gripped her child, this human child. "Merci, my child, are you okay?" the Queen inquired softly. Now, her maternal instincts were accurately aware of her daughter's inner turmoil.

"Yes, Mother," Merci said, startled from her contemplation, but the hesitation in her voice didn't escape her mother's notice. Sensing her daughter's unease, she probed further, "What troubles your heart, my dear?"

Merci's heart was filled with questions, and one weighed heavily on her. Summoning the courage to ask, Merci said, "Mother, once I transcended, will I still have the ability to have children?"

Antu, who understood the dynamics of transcendence, looked upon her daughter with a sad expression on her face. She knew that Merci's celestial form, bearing children was no longer possible. She began to explain, "Well, my child, after you've transcended, the celestial form you'll inhabit doesn't allow for the contraception of children unless you and your mate choose to take on human bodies temporarily for that purpose."

Merci's response seemed optimistic, "That's all simple enough?"

Antu knew better and said, "Yes, my dear, it may sound simple in theory, but in practice, it's far more complex."

As mother and daughter locked eyes, she couldn't help but notice the genuine confusion on Merci's face. Merci finally spoke, "I don't know what I'm feeling. I prayed to discover who I was, but now, with this newfound knowledge and the vast universe at my feet, I feel more lost and overwhelmed than ever. I'm heir to a kingdom I scarcely understand, and it's all so bewildering."

"As for the wedding, with a hint of secrecy, take all the time you need, my darling," Antu stopped her. This response was unexpected, adding an element of suspense to the conversation. Merci asked, "What about father?" She was taken aback by her mother's answer. Antu smiled at her daughter and said, "I will handle him." As Antu left Merci's chamber, she could feel the weight of her daughter's impending destiny. She knew that Merci needed time to come to terms with all that had been revealed, especially the daunting prospect of her Transcendence. Antu recognized the complexity of her daughter's emotions, a mix of curiosity, fear, and the overwhelming weight of responsibility.

Merci, left to her thoughts once again, realized that she was not altogether rejecting the idea of marriage; she simply needed more time to wrap her head around everything. Her mother's understanding and support were comforting. Enlil, with a sly and cunning smile, entered Merci's chamber, aware that he was walking a fine line between getting what he wanted and provoking his sister.

Merci was always on guard around him, yet curiously, she allowed him in, demanding to know his intentions. His excuse was that he was searching for Ishtar.

 Merci could sense there was more to it. Enlil claimed he wanted to assist Ishtar in capturing Asmodeus. Merci, perplexed, asked about the mysterious key and whether he planned to join Ishtar in battle.

Responses ladened with subtle accusations and insinuations, he questioned Merci's involvement in the demon's release onto earth, implying guilt on her part. He also tried to exploit her desire to prove herself, using her training by the goddess of war as leverage.

Seeing that his words were affecting her, Enlil pushed further, attempting to manipulate her emotions and judgment. Merci, irritated and feeling the pressure, snapped back at him, telling him to leave her alone. Leaving her chamber, he felt a sense of triumph.

He believed he could exploit Merci's vulnerabilities and use her for his own agenda, all while keeping her in the dark about his true intentions, adding more suspense to the brewing power struggle within the kingdom.

Merci, while amused by Enlil's arrogance, sensed that Enlil was up to something devious. She decided to follow him, using the skills she had learned from Asag, making herself nearly undetectable.

 She needed to uncover her brother's true intentions as she followed him.

Realizing that she would need a way to return to Earth discreetly, her starship would attract too much attention, so she opted for one of the nine gates, which allowed her to choose the time and place of her return carefully. She planned to return to Earth after her mysterious disappearance, hoping to find answers in that timeline.

Meanwhile, Ishtar had returned to Earth and continued to assist the detective in his investigations. The planet was in turmoil, with death and destruction becoming the norm. Governments were no longer serving the people, and many believed that the end of the days was at hand.

Asmodeus was relentless in his pursuit of the key; he knew that Ishtar was after it as well. This time, he was determined not to be stopped. The world tinkered on the edge of oblivion, and Ishtar's efforts were Earth's last hope, creating an atmosphere of ominous suspense.

Asmodeus, continuing his relentless pursuit of the key, was determined to stop at nothing until he found it. He knew that Ishtar was on Earth searching for him and the key. This time, he vowed not to be the one imprisoned.

Ishtar received an urgent message from the archangel Michael, who conveyed the importance of Yahweh's request for her presence. She immediately went to meet with Jesus, who was waiting for her in the throne room. After a warm welcome, He began to explain the reason for His summons. Jesus revealed that when He descended into hell, He had successfully retrieved the key. And in a hushed tone, He whispered the key's location to her, stressing the importance of guarding this information with her life. He explained that her mission was to retrieve the key and destroy it.

But there was more to the story; Jesus informed Ishtar about a special ring, the only thing capable of controlling Asmodeus and the demons that would soon threaten the earth. He narrated the tale of A Ring, A King, A Demon, and A remarkable temple. The ring had been presented to King Solomon by the Archangel Michael.

It bore engravings from God Himself, granting its wearer authority over both good and evil spirits, as well as dominion over animals, wind, and water. The story continues with the loss of the first ring to Asmodeus, who had tricked King Solomon into surrendering it, leading to Asmodeus's 40-year rule. The narrative was filled with suspense, setting the stage for the impending showdown with Asmodeus and the crucial mission to secure the key and the ring.

Continuing His narrative about the first ring, a magnificent creation made of pure iron and brass, covered in the purest gold and adorned with four precious jewels: a single Shimar Stone, a diamond, a ruby, and an emerald set in a six-point star—the Star of David.

He emphasized that the power of God resided within this ring and that it was the key to binding Asmodeus by branding the demon with the ring and uttering the words, "By the power of this seal, I commanded thee, and the demon would be compelled to obey."

Upon returning to Earth, Ishtar knew that time was of the essence; she needed to find Asmodeus as soon as possible and use the ring to stop him. To maintain her cover, she continues to live as Estelle's twin sister while secretly searching for Asmodeus.

Merci had planned to explore the universe. She longed to visit Orion and walk amongst the various species scattered throughout the cosmos. She was thirsty for more knowledge about the kingdom she was destined to rule and was eager to dig deeper into the Akashic records located in the realm of cosmic knowledge. Merci also sought to experience the repository of universal knowledge and to venture into the city of the gods.

Her research had unveiled information about the enigmatic nine gods, the creators of the nine principles that govern the universe. These beings held a significant place in the cosmic tapestry. Merci had embarked on a profound journey through the Universe and consulted with a multitude of diverse species. Among them, one individual stood out, Valiant Thor.

He introduced himself as a space emissary dispatched to Earth by the high council. Thor's mission was clear: to implore humanity to dismantle their nuclear arsenal. The council of the nine believed in granting mankind an opportunity to change their destructive path.

However, Thor's mission had ultimately failed, as the world's leaders, including President Eisenhower, were reluctant to disclose the truth to the public due to the military's opposition.

Thor had shared with Merci his observations of mankind's sensational hunger for war. Despite her intensive exploration of the universe, Merci couldn't shake off her preoccupation with Valiant Thor and his message about humanity. Her travels had broadened her perspective, but they had also intensified her concern about the state of the earth.

As she contemplated returning to earth, she was intercepted by her brother, Enki, who reminded her of the prohibition against her returning to the planet. Merci acknowledged this but expressed her strong conviction that there was something critical she needed to do on Earth. Her brother agreed, and as Merci and Enki prepared to descend to Earth, Enki confronted her about the prohibition of her return; however, she was resolute in her decision and revealed that their mother had tasked him with watching over her, to which she responded that he was now accompanying her.

Upon their return to Earth in the year 2013, Merci sensed an evil presence, which Enki identified as Asmodeus and his legions. The familiar surroundings didn't change, but the atmosphere felt distinctly different. Merci couldn't help but notice the tree outside her building was adorned with ribbons and well-wishing cards from both acquaintances as well as strangers, a testament to the care and concern people had for her.

As she entered the apartment building and passed by Fatima's neighboring apartment, she heard a baby crying. When she arrived at her apartment that she had once shared with Estelle, she heard mysterious sounds.

Knocking on the door, she was met with a surprised gaze from Ishtar. Understanding the sensitive nature of Merci's return, Ishtar signaled Merci and Enki to follow her lead. As they entered the apartment, they encountered a tall, handsome American detective fully engrossed in his work.

Looking up, he greeted Merci, saying, "Well, young lady," detective black began, "where have you been? The world has been looking for you. Can you tell me anything about where you've been for the past year?"

Merci paused momentarily, her memory still a confusing jumbo of the events of that day; she replied, "To be honest, I'm not sure; all I remember is I woke up in a cave, found my way to the closest city where I met this gentleman, I told him who I was, and he took me to his elders, and they sent me home."

Detective Black furrowed his brow, "so you don't remember anything?" "No, sir," Merci replied.

"Well, I'm sure you and your aunt have a lot to talk about," he said.

"I'll do my best to remember more," said Merci.

"Perhaps tomorrow, if you come to the station, you may be able to recall details that can help with the search for whatever your classmates released from that pyramid," said Detective Black.

As Ishtar escorted the detective to the door, she seethed with anger. She wanted to know why Merci was on Earth and how Enki could allow it. "Merci," Ishtar demanded upon returning to the room, "What are you doing? You know you're not supposed to be on earth in your present form. You have not transcended yet."

"Why, Auntie?" Merci said innocently, "I thought you and Enki were supposed to protect me."

"You know the consequences if anything happens to you, Merci," Ishtar said with a stern look.

"I'll be fine. I have you and my brother to look after me." Merci continued to look around, and her eyes fell upon the paperwork scattered on the table. "What's this?"

Ishtar sighed heavily. "I've been tracking Asmodeus, and I've narrowed down his whereabouts. He's about to uncover the location of the key," she said, her voice lowering to A hushed tone.

"Is there a way to reimprison him?" asked Merci

"Yes, there is," answered Ishtar. "But it's too dangerous for you," said Enki.

"Look, how am I going to know my powers if I'm not able to use them?" she questioned.

"You have not yet transcended, Merci; you can die here on Earth. If you die here before you transcend, you are surely

dead. It is important that I concentrate on finding Asmodeus and imprisoning him because if I do not, mankind cannot survive.

"Okay, so what's the next step? You must let me help you," said Merci, "I promise to be careful." Ishtar revealed, "The key was hidden in the Fertile Crescent, the birthplace of mankind; we must get it before he does. This location has two points in space connected by a gateway. This is where Jesus said he hid it."

"So how are we going to imprison him once we find him?" Merci asked. Enki said, "With the Ring of Solomon. Before we go to the location of the key, we must have Solomon's ring in our possession; it is the only thing left on earth that can imprison him."

"So where is it?" asked Merci.

"It's guarded by a sect called The Guardians of the Seal; the only problem is they went underground and haven't been seen nor heard from since Solomon's death. I have a lead on their possible location. That's where we must go first."

Their last location was inside Mount Hermon. Upon reaching Mount Hermon, they were met by an old man named Elias. His eyes showed ancient wisdom, and his demeanor eluded an aura of reverence. "Welcome travelers," Elias greeted, with his voice a gentle whisper, "for you seek the guardians of the seal, I presume?"

Ishtar nodded, "Yes. We need your assistance to retrieve the Ring of Solomon."

Elias studied them for a minute as if assessing their intent very well. He finally said, "Follow me." They entered the mountain through a concealed passage.

Once inside, they were struck with an otherworldly energy, and the walls seemed to pulse with hidden knowledge. Elias led them deeper into the caverns, where they finally reached a chamber bathed in a soft, ethereal light. Within this chamber, a group of individuals, each bearing an intricate seal on their robes, gathered in silent contemplation. These were the guardians of the seal, the protectors of the Ring of Solomon.

As they approached, Elias whispered something to the leader of the guardians, an elderly woman with eyes like ancient galaxies. She nodded, acknowledging their presence. "State your purpose," she demanded, her voice carrying the weight of centuries. Ishtar stepped forward, her determination unwavering, "We seek the Ring of Solomon to imprison Asmodeus; the fate of humanity depends on it."

The leader of the guardians regarded them for a moment, then nodded once more, "Very well! But retrieving the ring will not be easy. To prove your worth, you must first pass the trials of the seal."

"What trials?" Merci asked; her curiosity was piqued.

Elias turned to them, "These trials will test your resolve, your purity of heart, and your commitment to the cause. Only then will the guardians consider entrusting you with the ring."

With determination in their hearts, Ishtar, Merci, and Enki prepared to face the ancient trial that would determine their fate in the battle against the impending chaos that threatened to consume the world.

With time running out and the fate of Earth hanging in the balance, Ishtar, Merci, and Enki were determined to prove their worthiness to obtain Solomon's ring. They were led to the sacred trials set forth by the guardians of the seal, understanding that these challenges were the only path to acquiring the powerful artifact without delay. The trial of purity was the first trial that beckoned them into the heart of a mystical cabin, bathed in a soft, luminous glow of ancient crystals. They encountered a shimmering pool. Its Waters held the secrets of their true natures.

The elderly woman's voice resonated, "To pass this trial, you must cleanse your spirit of all the darkness and doubt. Only those of pure heart can proceed."

Without hesitation, Ishtar, Merci, and Enki stepped into the pool, surrendering themselves to its purifying magic. Their innermost being laid bare as they faced their own doubt, fears, and desires, seeking purity of intent.

The second trial, the trial of Resolve, unfolded on top of a treacherous mountain pass, where the winds howled with ominous intent. The path before them was a perilous ascent of towering cliffs. The man who had delivered them spoke sternly, "To prove your resolve, you must scale these cliffs together, relying on trust and unity. Only then will you reach the summit."

With unwavering trust and shared determination, they embarked on the ascent. Along the way, they confronted not only physical challenges but also their inner demons, which tested their unity. Together, they overcame each obstacle, reaching the summit as a United Force.

The third trial, the trial of Sacrifice, was conducted in a solemn chamber adorned with ancient symbols. They faced the third and final trial. At its center lay a gleaming dagger. The leader of the guardians explained solemnly, "To prove

your willingness to sacrifice for the greater good, one of
you must step forward, take up this dagger, and make a
symbolic offering."

As they exchanged glances filled with understanding,
Merci stepped forward without hesitation. She grasped the
dagger and made a symbolic Offering by slitting a cut into
the middle of her hand as the blood began to drip into the
ground; they now understood that it took their unwavering
commitment. They had successfully conquered all three
trials, and they returned to the guardian. Their spirits were
purified, their resolve unyielding, and their commitment
sealed in sacrifice.

The elderly woman nodded, ancient wisdom shining in her
eyes, "You have shown yourselves worthy. The Ring of
Solomon shall be entrusted to you when the time comes.
Now go forth and face the darkness that threatens your
world."

Armed with newfound strength and purpose, Ishtar, Merci,
and Enki set their sights on the impending battle against
Asmodeus, ready to do whatever it took to protect
humanity from the looming chaos, the trials proving their
worthiness to wield Solomon's ring.

As Enki soared over the Earth, witnessing the turmoil and chaos that had gripped humanity, he couldn't help but feel a profound sense of disappointment. This world, which he had once held in such high regard, had lost its way. It was he who had granted Prometheus the gift of fire, hoping to the flames of progress and enlightenment in the hearts of humankind. Yet, as he observed from above, it seemed that the very essence of his creation had been tainted by darkness.

Meanwhile, back at the Harlem residence, Merci and Ishtar were deeply engrossed in their strategic planning. They knew that a great battle lay ahead, and the fate of Earth hung precariously in the balance. That determination was unwavering as they worked tirelessly to prepare for the impending class with Asmodeus. However, their focused concentration was interrupted by an unexpected visitor, Fatima. She stood at the doorstep, cradling a baby boy in her arms.

Word had spread like wildfire that Merci had been found, and she had returned home. Her friends were gathering to welcome her. But when Merci saw the child in Fatima's embrace, her heart sank. His resemblance to Adonis was undeniable. Merci's reaction was immediate and visceral.

Hurt and betrayal welled inside her, and she couldn't contain her anguish. "How could you?" She cried out, "I thought you were my friend." Fatima desperately tried to explain, her words pouring out, but they fell on deaf ears. Merci had slammed the door shut, shutting out the voice of a former friend.

Inside, she grappled with the whirlwind of emotions. The pain and disappointment etched onto her face was plain to see, but her divine nature kept her from shedding tears. Instead, she pondered the truth about humanity, its greed and hatred. Her mind raced with questions about the love she once shared with Adonis, and doubts gnawed at her soul. Anger and confusion swirled within her, leaving her to wonder how someone she considered a friend could betray her so profoundly. These thoughts festered within Merci, stoking the fires of her anger. She was infuriated with herself for being so trusting, for believing in the inherent goodness of humanity.

As she contemplated the deceit, theft, and destruction she had witnessed, she began to question whether her mission to save humanity was even worth it. Perhaps she thought being a goddess was preferable to being entangled in a messy web of human affairs. *Were there any redeeming qualities in humanity?* she wondered, *"or had they become a species consumed by darkness?"*

Doubt gnawed at her; the allure of returning to Nibiru, getting married, and living out the remainder of her existence in the company of her kind beckoned. The line between her Divine and human side blurred, leaving her unsure of her own desires.

The moment for contemplation was over. It was time to confront Asmodeus, this malevolent force that threatened not only humanity but the very fabric of the universe. They had devised a plan. Merci would use her powers to confuse Asmodeus, while Ishtar would brand him with the seal, making him reimprison himself and all his evilness.

When they arrived, Asmodeus was waiting. A fierce battle erupted, an epic struggle that seemed to stretch into eternity. Powers clashed, the battle of good versus evil, and the very earth quaked under the intensity of their conflict. But when the dust settled, the demon Asmodeus was still at large, and he had his prize. Merci's life force had been drained to a mere flicker.

Ishtar wasted no time. Sending word to the child's mother and father, who rushed to her side as Asmodeus continued his reign of terror. The outcome was now at a critical juncture, and the fate of humanity was precautionarily poised. *Would she survive?* was the question. Enlil's next move was now to checkmate the King.